DRAFTED

— VOLUME I —

WRITER
MARK POWERS

LINE ARTIST
CHRIS LIE

COLOR ARTIST
JOSEPH BAKER

LETTERERS
CRANK! AND BRIAN J. CROWLEY

DESIGN
SEAN K. DOVE

EDITOR
MIKE O'SULLIVAN

For
Maryellen Powers
A truer hero there
never was.

DEVILS DUE PUBLISHING:

www.devilsdue.net

PRESIDENT **JOSH BLAYLOCK**
C.E.O. **PJ BICKETT**
ASSISTANT PUBLISHER **SAM WELLS**
ART DIRECTOR **SEAN DOVE**
MARKETING MANAGER **BRIAN WARMOTH**
SENIOR EDITOR **MIKE O'SULLIVAN**

I.P. DEVELOPMENT **STEPHEN CHRISTY**
STAFF ILLUSTRATOR **TIM SEELEY**
STAFF ILLUSTRATOR **MIKE BEAR**
WEBSTORE MANAGER **IDRIYS GRANT**
OFFICE ASSISTANCE **NORA HICKEY**
MANAGER OF FINANCE **DEBBIE DAVIS**

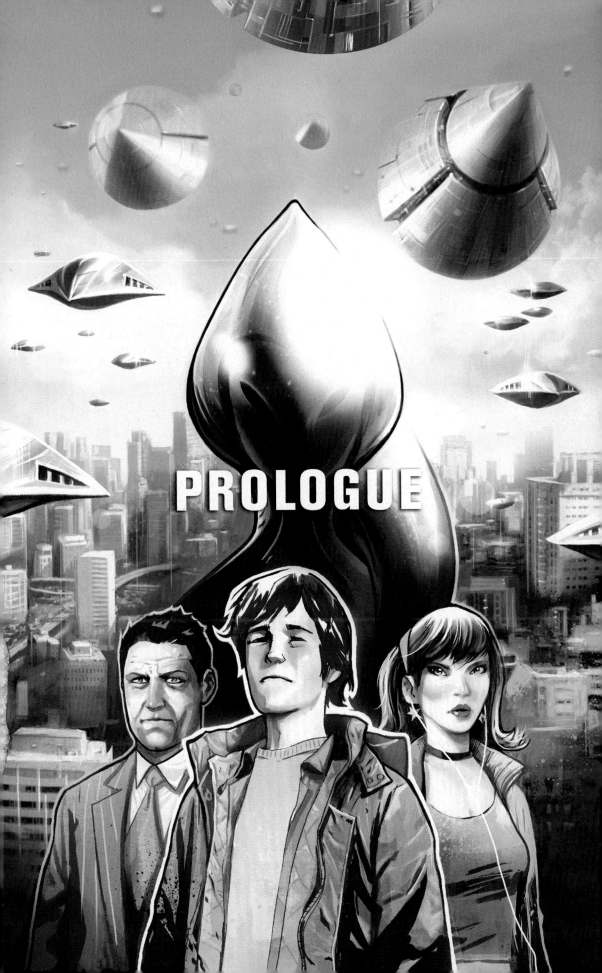

PROLOGUE

ST. LOUIS.

THREE DAYS LATER...

HOW *IS* SHE, KRIS?

IN *PAIN*, BUT STABLE--

--IN OTHER WORDS, JUST LIKE THE TWENTY *OTHERS* WE'VE PICKED UP TONIGHT.

YOU DON'T LOOK MUCH BETTER THAN *SHE* DOES.

YOU JUST STARTED *CHEMO* AGAIN A WEEK AGO.

SURE YOU'RE *UP* FOR THIS?

I'M *FINE*.

JESUS CHRIST!

THERE'S A GODDAMN *QUEUE* TO GET IN!

SOON...

HAVE YOU EVER *SEEN* ANYTHING LIKE THIS?

THEY SAY THE SAME THING HAPPENED IN ISRAEL.

WHAT THE HELL IS GOING *ON*, KRIS?

I DON'T KNOW, PARTNER--

--MAYBE GOD'S TRYING TO TELL US SOMETHING.

CHAPTER ONE:
THE AWAKENING

CLICK

BERLIN

THIS IS *HARRIS FERGUSON* REPORTING TO YOU LIVE FROM BERLIN--

--WHERE A MASSIVE *EARTHQUAKE* HAS WROUGHT UNIMAGINABLE DEATH AND DESTRUCTION.

AT THIS MOMENT, THOSE LUCKY ENOUGH TO HAVE ESCAPED HARM HAVE JOINED IN A DESPERATE ATTEMPT TO SAVE THE THOUSANDS TRAPPED UNDER THE *RUBBLE.*

C-CIVIL AUTHORITY HAS BROKEN *DOWN.* THE CHANCELLOR AND MUCH OF THE BUNDESTAG ARE BELIEVED DEAD...

WITH SCIENTISTS STILL MYSTIFIED BY THE ODD PHENOMENON THAT OCCURRED IN *ISRAEL* AND THE *UNITED STATES* LAST WEEK, AND THE EARTHQUAKE IN OTTAWA ONLY DAYS AGO--

--A GROWING NUMBER AROUND THE WORLD ARE BEGINNING TO SEE THE HAND OF A *GREATER* POWER IN THESE NATURAL DISASTERS.

WHATEVER THE CAUSE OF THESE EVENTS, *ONE* THING IS CERTAIN-- MORE HAVE DIED IN THE LAST WEEK THAN IN *ANY* SINGLE WEEK IN THE PAST SIXTY YEARS.

ONLY THROUGH AN UNPRECEDENTED LEVEL OF INTERNATIONAL COOPERATION CAN *FURTHER* LOSS OF LIFE BE *AVERTED.*

JESUS... ALL THOSE PEOPLE...

6:17 AM

RUNNING A LITTLE BIT *LATE* TODAY, VIC?

ACTUALLY, I HAVEN'T BEEN HOME SINCE *YESTERDAY.* WITH THE WORLD GOING NUTS, A FEW GUYS JUST STOPPED SHOWING *UP.*

NOBODY'S STOPPED THROWING AWAY *GARBAGE,* THOUGH. SO HERE I AM.

WHAT ABOUT *YOU,* KID? WHAT THE HELL ARE YOU STILL DOING IN DODGE?

NOBODY'S STOPPED BUYING CIGARETTES, COFFEE OR BEER.

FOR GOD'S SAKE, *GABRIEL*-- YOUR FATHER *DIED* BEHIND THAT COUNTER.

HE WANTED SOMETHING *BETTER* FOR YOU--

YOU THINK IT'S THAT *EASY,* VIC?

I'M NO *MILLIONAIRE.* I CAN'T PAY FOR SCHOOL, AND MY MOM *NEEDS* ME. BESIDES, THIS WAS MY FATHER'S JOB--

--I DON'T SEE ANY SHAME IN WHAT I DO. *SOMEBODY'S* GOT TO.

I DIDN'T MEAN TO SUGGEST IT'D BE *PAINLESS,* KID. JUST REMEMBER--

--AIN'T NOTHING IN LIFE WORSE THAN REGRET.

SEE YOU TOMORROW...

11:01 AM

THERE YOU GO, SHAREE.

IF YOU WIN, I HOPE THERE'S SOMETHING LEFT TO *SPEND* IT ON.

NOT WITH *MY* LUCK, HONEY.

1:57 PM

IT'S OKAY, MISS LOPES-- YOU PAY ME WHEN YOUR *CHECK* COMES IN. IT'LL BE OUR LITTLE SECRET.

YOU'RE A GOOD BOY, GABRIEL. *BLESSED.* REMEMBER, GOD LOVES THE COMPASSIONATE...

I'M SURE HE DOES, MISS LOPES. YOU JUST GET HOME SAFE.

5:01 PM

I'M TELLIN' YOU, I'M 21! GOT MY ID RIGHT HERE...

...I EXTEND THE *STRENGTH* AND *KINDNESS* OF THE AMERICAN PEOPLE TO OUR BROTHERS AND SISTERS IN GERMANY--

--KNOWING OUR SHARED LOVE OF FREEDOM WILL SEE US THROUGH THIS TERRIBLE CRISIS.

I *LOVE* THAT GUY. GREATEST *PRESIDENT* WE'VE EVER HAD.

UM... YEAH.

6:48 PM

TIME AND TIME AGAIN, AMERICA HAS PROVEN TO BE THE BEACON THAT CAN LEAD THE WORLD *OUT* OF DARKNESS--

--AND INTO THE LIGHT OF LIBERTY AND PROSPERITY.

GOD WILLING, WE WILL DO SO *AGAIN*.

PRESIDENT WALKER!

MR. PRESIDENT, IS IT TRUE THAT THE CHANCELLOR IS--

MR. PRESIDENT, HAVE YOU--

MR. PRESIDENT--

GO *AHEAD*, STRETCH.

MR. PRESIDENT, HAS ANY THOUGHT BEEN GIVEN TO DIVERTING *PERSONNEL* FROM THE MIDDLE EAST TO ASSIST WITH RELIEF EFFORTS IN GERMANY?

NO, I DON'T *GET* THOUGHTS.

THAT IS... YOU KNOW WHAT I MEAN.

WE'VE GOT THE RESOURCES TO DO *MORE* THAN ONE THING AT THE SAME TIME.

EXCUSE ME, SIR--

--MR. ADLEY NEEDS TO SEE YOU.

I'M AFRAID THE PRESIDENT'S ATTENTION IS URGENTLY NEEDED *ELSEWHERE* RIGHT NOW--

--GIVEN THE CIRCUMSTANCES, I'M SURE YOU *UNDERSTAND.* I'LL BE ANSWERING YOUR QUESTIONS IN HIS STEAD.

HOW'D I *SOUND*, STEPHAN?

COMMANDING, MR. PRESIDENT.

I DIDN'T *FEEL* COMMANDING.

IT FEELS LIKE I DON'T HAVE ANY CONTROL OVER *ANYTHING* ANYMORE.

WHAT THE HELL'S GOING *ON*, STEPH?

WE CAN'T ANSWER THAT JUST YET, SIR.

BUT WE'VE GOT THE WORLD'S TOP *GEOLOGISTS* STUDYING DATA FROM BERLIN AND OTTAWA, AND THEIR INITIAL FINDINGS ARE IN.

BOTH QUAKES REGISTERED *9-PLUS* ON THE RICHTER SCALE-- AND *NEITHER* REGION WAS KNOWN TO CONTAIN ANY SIGNIFICANT FAULT LINES.

WHAT... WHAT'S THE *DEATH TOLL* SO FAR...?

UNOFFICIALLY... OVER *EIGHTY THOUSAND* IN OTTAWA AND UPWARDS OF *TWO HUNDRED THOUSAND* IN BERLIN.

WE'RE STILL TRYING TO ASCERTAIN HOW MANY *MORE* ARE MISSING OR HOMELESS. *DISEASE* IS BEGINNING TO BECOME A CONCERN, TOO.

MY GOD.

BETTER NEWS FROM ST. LOUIS AND JERUSALEM. STILL NO FATALITIES IN THE AFTERMATH OF *THE PHENOMENON*--

--OUR BEST GUESS IS THAT A SUDDEN DROP IN AIR PRESSURE WAS RESPONSIBLE FOR THE MILD PHYSICAL EFFECTS EXPERIENCED BY THE LOCAL POPULATIONS.

SUBJECTS HERE AND IN ISRAEL WILL BE RELEASED FROM QUARANTINE SHORTLY.

STILL.... THERE'S A LOT OF *FEAR* OUT THERE. BETWEEN ALL THESE NATURAL DISASTERS, AND THE USUAL WARS AND POLITICAL UPHEAVALS... PEOPLE ARE DESPERATE FOR SOMETHING TO GRAB *HOLD* OF.

THEY WANT *LEADERSHIP*, STEPH. AND *I'M* GOING TO GIVE IT TO THEM.

THIS IS WHY I WAS *PUT* HERE. *THIS* IS WHY I BECAME PRESIDENT.

IT'S MY *DESTINY*.

QUARANTINE ZONE

A JEWISH SOLDIER--

ASK HIM WHY WE'RE BEING HELD--

EXCUSE ME... MANY PARDONS...

NASR...? *NASR!*

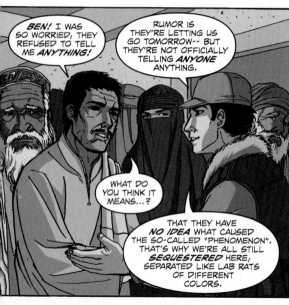

BEN! I WAS SO WORRIED, THEY REFUSED TO TELL ME *ANYTHING!*

RUMOR IS THEY'RE LETTING US GO TOMORROW-- BUT THEY'RE NOT OFFICIALLY TELLING *ANYONE* ANYTHING.

WHAT DO YOU THINK IT MEANS...?

THAT THEY HAVE *NO IDEA* WHAT CAUSED THE SO-CALLED "PHENOMENON", THAT'S WHY WE'RE ALL STILL *SEQUESTERED* HERE, SEPARATED LIKE LAB RATS OF DIFFERENT COLORS.

AT LEAST IT SEEMS THERE HAVE BEEN NO *LASTING* EFFECTS... HAVE YOU SPOKEN TO YOUR *SARAH?*

THEY ALLOWED ME *ONE* PHONE CALL. SHE'S FINE, BUT *SCARED.* I THINK *EVERYONE* IS-- MY SUPERIORS MORE THAN ANYONE.

WELL, NO ONE KNOWS BETTER THAN THE JEW OR PALESTINIAN WHAT *FEAR* DOES TO A PEOPLE.

I SEE YOU'VE NOTICED MY *FRIEND!* *YES,* HE'S JEWISH. *NO,* HE'S NOT HERE TO DEVOUR YOUR YOUNG.

HE *DOES* HAVE A DREADFUL *SMOKING* HABIT, HOWEVER, SO BEWARE YOUR CIGARETTES!

MY FRIEND, I SENSE POLITICS IN YOUR FUTURE.

⟨ THERE. ⟩*

*TRANSLATED FROM THE PASHTO. --MIKE

⟨ SOHILA, *YOU* WILL COME WITH ME. WE DO THIS *QUIETLY.* AND DO NOT HESITATE TO *SHOOT* IF YOU ENCOUNTER RESISTANCE-- ⟩

⟨ --YOU *KNOW* WHAT THEY'LL DO TO US IF WE'RE CAPTURED. ⟩

⟨ THIS IS THE BUILDING. THEY HAVE THIRTY SECONDS TO DECIDE WHETHER OR NOT THEY'RE *COMING.* ⟩

⟨ THEY *TAKE* NOTHING WITH THEM. THEY SAY NO *GOODBYES.* DO YOU UNDERSTAND? ⟩

⟨ YES, *RAISA.* ⟩

⟨ BE SILENT! ⟩

⟨ WE ARE HERE TO *FREE* YOU. ⟩

⟨ THE TULLAAB HAVE MADE YOU SLAVES! THIS IS *NOT* AS NATURE INTENDED US. ⟩

⟨ *COME* WITH ME, AND YOU WILL BE FREE-- TO *THINK.* TO *ACT.* TO DO AS YOU *PLEASE!* ⟩

⟨ BUT YOU MUST DECIDE NOW. THERE IS NO TIME FOR *DEBATE*-- ⟩

⟨ WHAT IS *HAPPENING* HERE?! ⟩

⟨ WHO *ARE* YOU, WOMAN? ⟩

< I AM YOUR GREATEST *FEAR*, ZEALOT-- A FEMALE WITH A *MIND*. >

< WE EXPECTED ARMED GUARDS. WHERE ARE THE *OTHER* MEN? >

< ANY OF THESE WOMEN WHO DESIRE IT ARE COMING *WITH* ME. >

< OUR TEACHERS... HAVE BEEN *DISTRACTED*. THEY SPEND THEIR DAYS DEBATING THE *MEANING* OF RECENT EVENTS. >

< THEY FEAR GOD'S JUDGMENT. >

< AS WELL THEY *SHOULD*. >

< BEFORE WE ABANDON YOU TO YOUR IGNORANCE, YOU MUST ANSWER ONE *QUESTION*-- >

< --HAVE YOU SEEN THIS GIRL? >

< SHE'D BE *SEVENTEEN* NOW. >

< N-NO... I DO NOT RECOGNIZE HER. >

< THEN... WE WILL TAKE OUR *LEAVE*. >

< WE WILL FIND YOUR *DAUGHTER*, RAISA. I *KNOW* IT. >

< I WANT TO BELIEVE YOU. I WANT TO *PRAY* FOR HER SAFE RETURN... >

< ...BUT I JUST DON'T HAVE ANY *FAITH* LEFT. >

--DEATH TOLL HAS CLIMBED TO OVER EIGHTY THOUSAND IN OTTAWA. NOW, ANOTHER EARTHQUAKE HAS *DEVASTATED* ONE OF EUROPE'S MOST HISTORIC CITIES.

MORNING, ALL!

LITTLE REMAINS OF BERLIN, AND HOPE IS FADING FOR THE THOUSANDS STILL TRAPPED IN THE RUBBLE.

MEANWHILE, AMERICAN SECRETARY OF STATE CAROLYN LANE WILL ARRIVE TODAY IN MONTREAL FOR AN EMERGENCY CONFERENCE WITH PRIME MINISTER HARPER--

MAYBE YOU'RE NOT KEEPING UP ON CURRENT EVENTS, *AUDREY*, BUT ALMOST HALF A MILLION PEOPLE HAVE *DIED* IN THE LAST WEEK.

YOU MIGHT WANT TO TONE DOWN YOUR USUAL ACT AND PRETEND YOU *CARE*.

I SUPPOSE I SHOULD ADAPT *YOUR* USUAL DOUR PERSONALITY, STEVE? WOULD *THAT* SHOW I CARE?

YOU HAVE NO *IDEA* HOW I FEEL, AND NO *RIGHT* TO JUDGE ME.

SEEING ALL THE CRAP THAT'S HAPPENING IN THE WORLD NOW JUST MAKES ME APPRECIATE EVERY SECOND THAT MUCH *MORE*.

YEAH...

...YOU'RE A REAL INSPIRATION,

...THERE IS A REAL SENSE THAT THE WORLD HAS CHANGED *IRREVOCABLY*, THAT *NOTHING* WILL EVER BE THE SAME...

IT'S TIME TO BE REALISTIC, KRIS.

YOU CAN'T DO THIS ANYMORE.

DO WHAT? LAY IN A HOSPITAL BED? YOU'RE DAMN RIGHT I CAN'T DO THAT, COLIN.

YOU KNOW WHAT I MEAN.

YOU HAVE CANCER, KRIS. CANCER!

AND YET YOU'RE RUNNING AROUND LIKE MOTHER TERESA, TRYING TO SAVE THE WORLD.

YOU'VE BEEN AN EMT FOR FIVE YEARS NOW. HOW MANY LIVES HAVE YOU SAVED IN ALL THAT TIME?

TIME TO SAVE YOURSELF. IT'S TIME TO QUIT... TO GIVE YOUR BODY A FIGHTING CHANCE TO BEAT THIS DISEASE.

NO.

AIN'T NO CURE FOR WHAT I HAVE. THE BEST I CAN HOPE FOR IS TO BEAT IT INTO REMISSION EVERY FEW MONTHS.

I'M TIRED OF THAT CYCLE.

LET'S FACE FACTS, COL-- I'M GOING TO DIE. I MAY AS WELL HELP AS MANY PEOPLE AS I CAN ALONG THE WAY. IT'S WHAT I'VE ALWAYS BEEN BEST AT.

CHIN UP, BRO'...

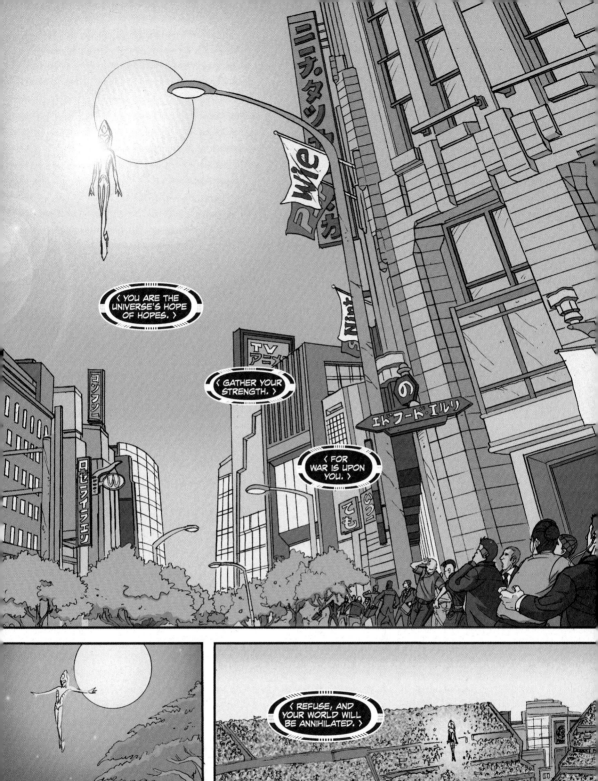

"THIS CANNOT BE DECIDED *UNILATERALLY!*"

THESE BEINGS ADDRESSED *EVERYONE* ON EARTH SIMULTANEOUSLY. *I* HEARD SWAHILI. *YOU* HEARD ENGLISH.

WHAT IS HAPPENING AFFECTS ALL PEOPLE *EQUALLY*-- WHY DO YOU REFUSE TO SEE *REASON?*

THE ERA OF THE WEST DOMINATING THE REST OF THE WORLD IS *OVER!*

AND YOU SHOULD SEE THAT THIS IS TOO DAMNED *IMPORTANT* TO PLAY PRETEND DIPLOMACY--

--THIS DECISION NEEDS TO BE LEFT TO THE NATIONS WHO'VE THE MOST *EXPERIENCE* WAGING WAR AND SETTLING THE PEACE!

YOU *DO* HAVE MORE EXPERIENCE WAGING WAR-- ON POORER NATIONS.

THAT POINT I WILL NOT ARGUE!

COME OFF IT--

WHY ARE WE EVEN *ARGUING?* THIS IS THE MOST *SIGNIFICANT* EVENT IN HUMAN HISTORY-- SHOULDN'T WE TRY TO MAKE *PEACE* WITH THESE BEINGS?

PEACE--? "THESE BEINGS" *MUST* BE RESPONSIBLE FOR THE RECENT EARTHQUAKES.

IF WE ACQUIESCE, *HUMAN HISTORY* IS AT AN END--

THAT IS TRUE NO MATTER *WHAT* COURSE WE CHOOSE.

IS THIS WHO WE ARE? ARE WE REALLY THIS *WEAK?!*

I SAID--

--*IS THIS WHO WE ARE?!*

PRESTON

HUMANITY'S LIVED THROUGH *FLOODS.* *FAMINE.* GLOBAL *CONFLICT.*

WE'VE CURED DEADLY *DISEASES.* WE'VE *CROSSED* OCEANS, *RAISED* CITIES, EVEN VISITED THE *MOON.*

WE'VE *CONQUERED* EVERYTHING *NATURE* COULD POSSIBLY THROW AT US.

WE MAY FIGHT AMONGST *OURSELVES,* YES. FAR TOO *OFTEN.*

BUT THERE IS ONE THING I KNOW WE'LL *NEVER DO--*

--AND THAT'S *BOW!*

LOOK, LET'S JUST ADMIT IT... WE'RE ALL *SCARED.* SCARED *SHITLESS.*

BUT *THINK* ABOUT IT-- *THEY* CAME TO *US.* THAT MEANS THEY *NEED* US.

MAYBE WHERE *THEY* COME FROM, IT'S NORMAL TO MAKE DEMANDS ON THE PLAYER WHO HOLDS ALL THE *CARDS--*

--BUT WHERE I WAS RAISED, WE DON'T COTTON TO THAT.

AS AN *AMERICAN,* I BELIEVE IN MAN'S SPECIAL DESTINY--

--THAT THIS WORLD BELONGS TO *US* BY *DIVINE RIGHT.*

DO ANY OF YOU WANT TO LOOK AT YOUR CHILDREN-- AND HAVE THEM KNOW *YOU* ALLOWED THEIR WORLD TO BE *TAKEN* FROM THEM?

IF WE GIVE IN TO THESE--THESE *THINGS,* WE WILL HAVE ACCEPTED SLAVERY!

I ASK *EACH* OF YOU. AS INDIVIDUALS-- AS *REPRESENTATIVES* OF YOUR PEOPLES--

--ARE YOU *SLAVES?!*

NAY!

RESIST!

NO!.

NEVER!

NEVER!

NO!

NO!

THEN LET US SEND THE MESSAGE *OUT.* IN EVERY *LANGUAGE,* OVER EVERY *FREQUENCY.*

NEGOTIATE WITH US AS EQUALS, AND SECURE OUR AID-- OR SUFFER OUR *WRATH.*

AND IF OUR VISITORS CHOOSE *THAT* PATH... WELL, THEN, *BRING IT ON!*

"--WITHIN THE NEXT FEW DAYS, OUR SPECIES WILL EITHER TAKE A GIANT LEAP FORWARD...OR CEASE TO EXIST."

LOOK AT THEM, NASR. ISN'T... ISN'T IT *BEAUTIFUL?*

OUR PEOPLE... PRAYING *TOGETHER.*

WHY COULDN'T IT BE LIKE THIS *BEFORE...?*

WE *WERE* LIKE THIS BEFORE. *YOU* AND *I.*

IT'S ALMOST FUNNY. TO SURVIVE ALL THE *HATRED* AND BLOODSHED, ONLY TO FACE *THIS...*

CAN THIS REALLY BE *HAPPENING?*

IT'S *HAPPENING,* CHAZER!

I PRAY SARAH MADE IT TO HER MOTHER'S SAFELY... I'LL NEVER GET TO HER THROUGH--

RRRRR...UMMMBLE

WH-WHAT WAS *THAT?!*

PLEASE, NOT AN *EARTHQUAKE...* NOT *HERE!*

IT WAS *NOTHING...* PROBABLY JUST CAUSED BY THE SHEER SIZE OF THE *CROWD...* RIGHT?

FROM YOUR MOUTH TO GOD'S EARS.

NO, PLEASE NO...

RRRRRRRR...HMMMMBLE

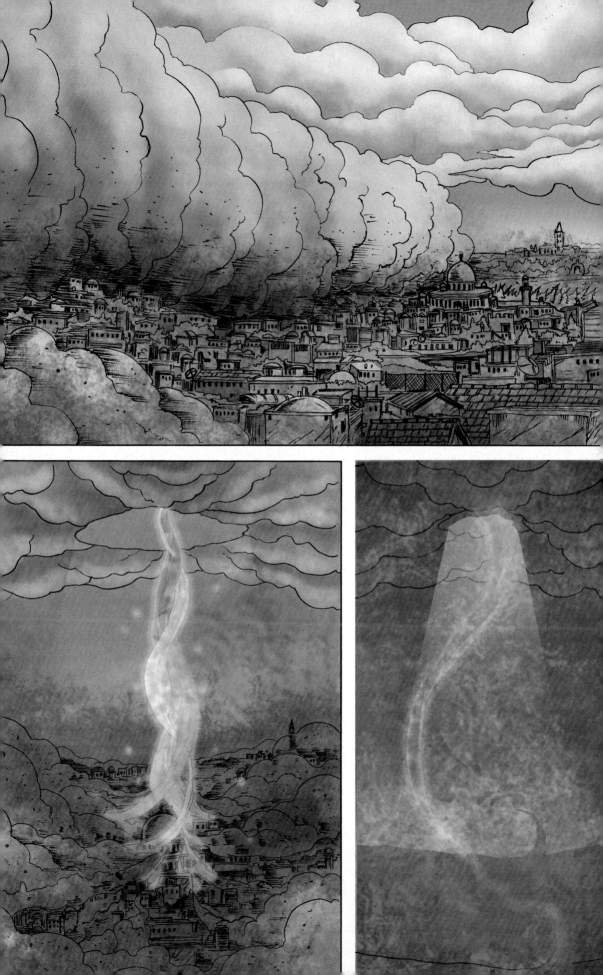

W-WE HAVE BEEN UNABLE TO *COMMUNICATE* WITH ANYONE INSIDE JERUSALEM...

...AND V-VIOLENT WEATHER CONDITIONS IN THE AREA HAVE PREVENTED US FROM EVEN SURVEYING THE SCENE FROM THE *AIR.*

MY FRIENDS... N-NOW, MORE THAN EVER, THE JEWISH PEOPLE NEED YOUR *HELP.*

IS THIS... THE ALIENS' *RESPONSE* TO THE U.N.'S MESSAGE?

WHAT THE HELL *ELSE* COULD IT BE, GENERAL?

THE QUESTION IS-- WHAT DO WE DO *NOW?* WHAT *CAN* WE DO?

WE CAN HELP OUR *FRIENDS.*

MR. PRESIDENT, *JORDAN* AND *EGYPT* HAVE ALREADY VOLUNTEERED UNLIMITED MANPOWER AND MATERIAL AID TO ISRAEL.

WE NEED TO DO THE *SAME.*

MR. PRESIDENT...?

YES. SEND THEM WHATEVER THEY *NEED.*

ISRAEL.

OUR *SATELLITES* HAVE MADE SEVERAL PASSES OVER THE CITY, BUT WE'VE BEEN UNABLE TO PENETRATE THE WEATHER COVERAGE.

DO YOU HAVE A *VISUAL* YET, MAJOR?

NEGATIVE, WASHINGTON. NOT EVEN ON INFRARED. BUT WE SHOULD BE CLOSE TO THE HEART OF THE CITY NOW...

"SHOULD BE"?

THERE'S JUST... IT'S ALL... SAND. LIKE A *DESERT.*

THAT... THAT MAKES NO *SENSE!*

WHAT *HAS* MADE SENSE IN THE LAST FORTY-EIGHT HOURS?

MAJOR! LOOK--!

MY GOD.

MAJOR, WHAT IS IT? WHAT DO YOU *SEE...?*

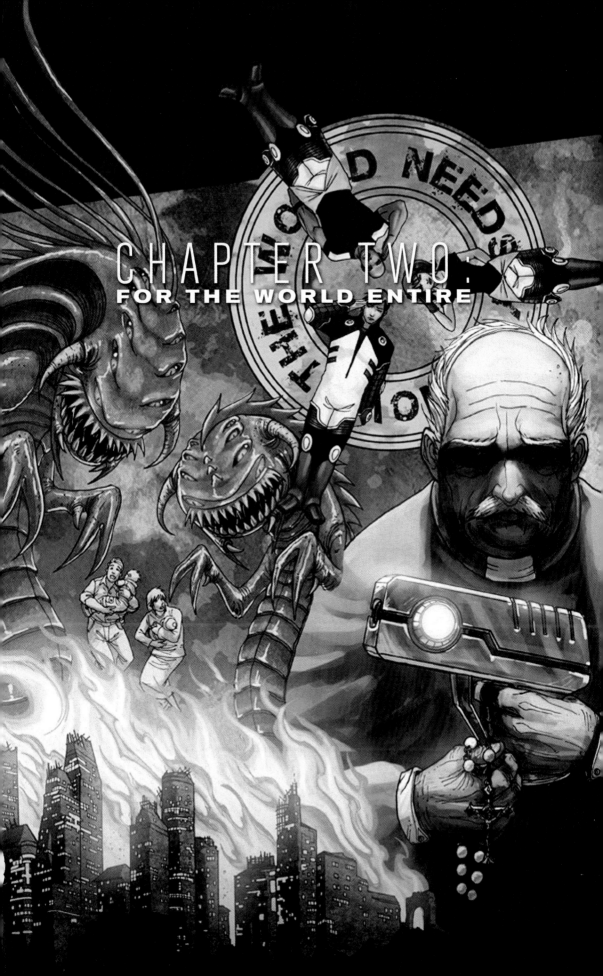

CHAPTER TWO:
FOR THE WORLD ENTIRE

ISRAEL

⟨INFRARED SATELLITE SCANS INDICATE NO SIGNIFICANT SIGNS OF LIFE--⟩*

⟨ENERGY LEVELS ARE OFF THE *CHARTS*--⟩

⟨OVER HERE! *OVER HERE!* I THINK--⟩

* TRANSLATED FROM THE HEBREW.

⟨--I THINK I'VE FOUND OUR FIRST *BODY.*⟩

⟨MY GOD! IT-IT'S BEEN SEVERED IN *HALF!* WHAT THE HELL *HAPPENED* HERE?!⟩

⟨WE CAN'T ANSWER THAT YET, SIR. ALL WE *DO* KNOW IS THAT *JERUSALEM,* AND ALL ITS INHABITANTS--⟩

IT'S NOT YOUR FAULT, *PRESTON.*

I KNOW.

DO I...? WHO *ELSE'S* FAULT COULD IT BE?

ALIENS. MY GOD... ALIENS! THIS ISN'T *REAL.* IT *CAN'T* BE REAL!

HOW COULD EVERYTHING HAVE CHANGED SO *QUICKLY?*

WHY AM I *HERE?* WHY DID I *CHOOSE* THIS LIFE...?

DID I *EVER* REALLY WANT IT-- OR DID I *WANT* TO WANT IT...?

GOD, WHAT DO I DO NOW? WHAT DO I *DO?*

PRESTON... *NO ONE* COULD HAVE KNOWN WHAT WOULD HAPPEN.

STOP IT. STOP TEARING YOURSELF APART.

HOW CAN SHE STILL *BELIEVE* IN ME? AFTER EVERY FUCK UP... EVERY *FAILURE?*

LORI, I...

I WAS JUST TRYING TO BE *STRONG.* TO ACT LIKE A PRESIDENT'S *SUPPOSED* TO ACT.

JESUS. ALL THOSE *PEOPLE...*

THOSE... THOSE *THINGS* DID THAT. NOT *YOU.*

NOT YOU.

EXCUSE ME, MR. PRESIDENT--

--YOU'RE GOING TO WANT TO TURN ON THE *TELEVISION.*

NOW WHAT THE HELL...?

KLIK

--DEVELOPING CRISIS IN TEL AVIV THREATENS TO *PROVOKE* THE EXTRATERRESTRIALS FURTHER.

CCN — LIVE

IN THE CHAOTIC AFTERMATH OF JERUSALEM'S DESTRUCTION, ISRAELI AIR FORCE COLONEL *GIORA SHALIACH*, WHO LOST HIS *ENTIRE FAMILY* IN THE ATTACK--

--HAS TAKEN OFF IN A *NESHER* JETFIGHTER WITHOUT *AUTHORIZATION.*

HIS AIM, APPARENTLY, IS TO STRIKE *BACK* AT THE STRANGE VESSEL LOOMING OVER HIS COUNTRY.

CCN

STOCK PHOTO

FEARING EVEN GREATER *REPRISALS* FROM THE ALIENS, THE ISRAELI AIR FORCE ORDERED FIGHTERS SCRAMBLED TO *PURSUE* HIM--

--BUT COLONEL SHALIACH'S FELLOW PILOTS *REFUSED.*

SO NOW, THE WORLD CAN ONLY WATCH...

...AND PRAY.

WOODSIDE, NEW YORK

THANK YOU, HARRIS. IN A MOMENT, WE'LL BE TALKING AGAIN WITH *DR. DEVON McNEIL* TO GET HER TAKE ON THE *PSYCHOLOGICAL* RAMIFICATIONS OF THESE HISTORIC EVENTS--

IT'S OKAY, MOMMA, EVERYTHING'S GOING TO BE OKAY...

GABRIEL WILL TAKE CARE OF US.

...POR LOS SIGLOS DE LOS SIGLOS, AMEN...

GABRIEL...?

WHAT...? SORRY, LUCIA.

YOU KNOW I'LL ALWAYS WATCH OVER MY TWO GIRLS.

OH MI JESUS, PERDÓNANOS NUESTROS PECADOS...

MOMMA, CAN I GET YOU ANYTHING?

MOM--

SHE'S *NOT* GOING TO ANSWER YOU. SHE'S TOO OUT OF IT.

GABRIEL, *PLEASE.* T-TELL ME THE *TRUTH.*

ARE... ARE WE GOING TO *DIE?*

HEY.

HEY. DON'T *SAY* THAT.

LOOK... I'M AS *SCARED* AS YOU ARE. AND I CAN'T PROMISE YOU THAT... WELL, THAT EVERYTHING'S GOING TO TURN OUT *OKAY.*

BUT... I LOVE YOU, LUC'.

I'LL *ALWAYS* WATCH OUT FOR YOU, AS BEST I CAN. NO MATTER *WHAT.*

NOW C'MON.

LET'S GO MAKE MA SOME TEA, LIKE WHEN WE WERE *KIDS.* EXTRA SUGAR AND ALL.

GABRIEL...?

YEAH, LUC'?

SHHHHH, LUC'. WHATEVER HAPPENS, IT'LL HAPPEN TO US *TOGETHER.*

PROMISE...

...NO OFFICIAL WORD YET REGARDING THE EXACT NUMBER OF CASUALTIES IN JERUSALEM...

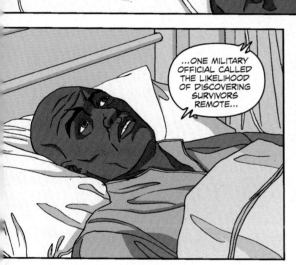

...ONE MILITARY OFFICIAL CALLED THE LIKELIHOOD OF DISCOVERING SURVIVORS REMOTE...

WHAT THE...?

...COMING UP, WE'LL BE SPEAKING LIVE TO NASA'S DIRECTOR, WHO'LL TRY TO EXPLAIN WHY WE DIDN'T DETECT THEIR APPROACH...

THIS IS IMPOSSIBLE. IT CAN'T BE...

I'M...

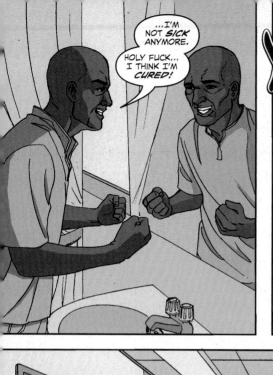

...I'M NOT *SICK* ANYMORE.

HOLY FUCK... I THINK I'M *CURED!*

YAAAHHHHH!

BELIEVE IT, MAN. BELIEVE IT!

WE'RE *HEALED!*

IT'S A *MIRACLE!*

WOO-HOOO!

PLEASE, UNTIL THE DOCTOR CAN *EXAMINE* EVERYONE, YOU'VE ALL GOT TO STAY CALM!

IT WAS *THEM,* NURSE STEVENS. IT *HAD* TO BE.

THE ALIENS! *THEY'VE CURED US!*

...BREAKING NEWS-- WE INTERRUPT WITH WHAT IS APPARENTLY A TRANSMISSION...

CCN EXCLUSIVE

BREAKING NEWS

CCN

...DIRECTLY FROM THE ROGUE ISRAELI PILOT, COLONEL SHALIACH. S-STAND BY...

CCN EXCLUSIVE

BREAKING NEWS

CCN

...I'M TRANSMITTING OVER ALL CHANNELS AND FREQUENCIES--

--THIS WILL BE MY *FINAL* MESSAGE.

WHAT I DO NOW, I DO NOT ONLY FOR MY FAMILY AND MY *PEOPLE,* BUT THE WORLD *ENTIRE.*

I KNOW YOU FEAR WHAT THESE BEINGS WILL DO IN RETALIATION, BUT I...

I COULD NOT ALLOW THEIR CRIME TO GO *UNCHALLENGED.*

I PRAY *OTHERS* WILL FOLLOW MY EXAMPLE--

WHAT THE-?

MY GOD.

‹THEY KILLED HIM!› *

* TRANSLATED FROM MANDARIN.

‹...WE BELIEVE... WE BELIEVE WHAT YOU JUST HEARD LIVE... WAS THE DEATH OF COLONEL SHALIACH...›

‹HE WAS TRYING TO AVENGE HIS FAMILY, AND THEY FUCKING KILLED HIM!›

‹HOW CAN YOU SIT THERE STUFFING YOUR FACE?›

AGGHH!

BLAM!

KA-SPAK!

TZZAAK!

‹WHAT THE HELL!?›

‹STOP SNIVELING.›

‹AND LET ME SAVE YOU THE SUSPENSE-- WE ARE GOING TO DIE, TOO.›

‹PROBABLY PAINFULLY.›

‹THE QUESTION IS, FOR ONCE IN YOUR MISERABLE, MISSPENT LIVES--

‹--ARE YOU WILLING TO FIGHT FOR SOMETHING LARGER THAN YOURSELVES?›

‹TEAMING UP WITH A DAMNED COP. THE WORLD MUST BE ENDING. HOW DO WE DO THIS?›

‹I KNOW FOR A FACT YOU HAVE... ASSOCIATES WHO CAN HELP WITH ARMAMENTS.›

‹AND WE WILL FIND WILLING ALLIES IN THE MILITARY AND SCIENTIFIC COMMUNITIES.›

‹BUT WE MUST ACT QUICKLY...›

IT'S ALL A *LIE!*

THAT-- THAT *BOOK* YOU HOLD UNDER YOUR ARM. NOTHING BUT *LIES!*

THERE *IS* NO GOD!

JAMAAL!

DON'T BEGRUDGE HIM HIS ANGER. IF WE NEVER FELT *DOUBT,* WE WOULDN'T BE HUMAN.

DO YOU THINK PART OF *ME* DOESN'T FEEL THE SAME?

BUT THESE CREATURES, IMAM. DOESN'T THEIR *EXISTENCE* CONTRADICT EVERYTHING WE'VE BEEN TAUGHT?

AND IF THERE *IS* A GOD--

"IF THERE IS A GOD, HOW COULD HE ALLOW THE DEATHS OF MILLIONS?"

THE SAME WAY HE "ALLOWS" WAR, FAMINE, AND DISEASE. HIS NATURE IS *BEYOND* OUR KNOWING.

BELIEVING EVERY WORD IN THIS BOOK TO BE *LITERAL* TRUTH IS, ULTIMATELY, POINTLESS--

--ITS POWER COMES FROM THE MORAL CODE IT GIVES US. CAN *THAT* EVER REALLY BE INVALIDATED?

THE KORAN SAYS "ALL PEOPLE ARE A SINGLE NATION".

TIME FOR US TO *PROVE* IT.

AUDREY...?

AUDREY!

HEY, GIRL!

TOM?

HOW COME YOU'RE NOT OUT IN THE *MIDDLE* OF ALL THIS? IT'S THE END OF THE WORLD! TIME TO LET IT ALL HANG OUT, SODOM AND GOMORRAH STYLE!

JUST TAKING A BREATHER! YOU KNOW ME-- I'M *ALWAYS* READY TO PARTY!

COOL, YOU HAD ME WORRIED FOR A SEC! ANYWAY, I...

I JUST WANTED TO *APOLOGIZE* FOR THE WAY WE ALL ACTED TOWARDS YOU THE OTHER DAY!

FORGET IT! LISTEN, I'LL CATCH YOU IN A FEW! GOTTA GET SOME AIR!

=SNIFF=
SORRY...
SO SORRY.

CAN'T *DO*
THIS ANYMORE...
I JUST CAN'T...

ALYIA...
PLEASE.
PLEASE
FORGIVE
ME...

YOU WERE SO CUTE! *LOOK* AT YOU IN YOUR LITTLE BATMAN COSTUME!

YEAH, MY *HOMEMADE* COSTUME.

KIDS AT SCHOOL *LOVED* THAT. I WAS THE LAUGHINGSTOCK OF THE THIRD GRADE HALLOWEEN PARTY.

'MEMBER HOW *DADDY* USE TO TAKE US TRICK OR TREATING IN FOREST HILLS?

HE SAID WE'D GET A BETTER *HAUL* THERE. ALWAYS MADE SEEM LIKE SOME GREA ADVENTURE, DIDN'T HE...?

I *MISS* HIM. ESPECIALLY NOW...

YEAH, ME TOO.

YOU LOOK LIKE HIM, GABRIEL... YOU *REMIND* ME OF HIM.

HE'D BE *PROUD* OF YOU, THE WAY YOU'VE ALWAYS TAKEN CARE OF US.

...

I'M GONNA GET SOME MORE TEA... YOU WANT SOME?

SURE. DON'T FORGET THE EXTRA SUGAR.

HEH. *HERE'S* ONE OF DADDY CHANGING YOUR DIAPER.

DADDY...

KRSH!

WHA--!?

GABRIEL? W-WHAT *WAS* THAT?

GABRIEL...?

OH... OHMIGOD!

GABRIEL!

<--THIS IS ONLY THE BEGINNING.>

<OUR PRIORITY NOW IS TO MAKE SURE EVERY ABLE BODIED MAN IS *ARMED*.>

<HELL, THE WOMEN, TOO.>

<WE'RE NOT LOSING THIS PLANET WITHOUT A *FIGHT*.>

<THIS IS AN EXCELLENT *START*. BUT WE'RE GOING TO NEED MORE POWERFUL--->

<WHAT THE F--->

SOMEONE'S CUT THE *POWER*--

<IT'S *THEM*!>

BLAM! GRRRCH!

NOoo!!

AIEEEE!

BLAM!

<DAMNED FILTHY =NNNNNGGHHΞ>

WHY?

WHY COULDN'T YOU *WAIT*? YOU WOULD HAVE SEEN THAT WE ONLY SEEK TO *PROTECT* YOU.

MAY YOUR SPIRITS FORGIVE ME.

SHHH, PRESTON... IT'S GOING TO BE OKAY.

I-I DON'T THINK HE HEARS YOU, LORI. HE'S TOTALLY *OUT* OF IT.

HE'S BETTER THAN WHAT PEOPLE *THINK*, YOU KNOW. HE MEANS WELL...

GOOD INTENTIONS DON'T MEAN *ANYTHING* WHEN THEY'RE COMPROMISED BY BLIND CERTAINTY.

SHIT, WHO AM I TO TALK? I THINK IT'S SAFE TO SAY WE'RE *ALL* GOING TO HAVE OUR FAILINGS EXPOSED IN THE DAYS TO COME.

IF WE *HAVE* "DAYS", THAT IS...

LOOK, I NEED TO GO MEET WITH THE VICE PRESIDENT. LET ME KNOW IF YOU *NEED* ANYTHING.

THANK YOU, STEPHAN.

WHAT THE--?!

STEPHAN!

STEPHAN!

NOOOOOOO!

LORI--?! *WHERE'S* THE PRESIDENT?

HE'S *GONE*, STEPHAN! H-HE JUST... JUST *DISAPPEARED!*

〈COLONEL SHALIACH!〉

〈B-BUT HOW...?!〉

〈LISTEN.〉

〈YOU NEED TO TAKE ME TO *HEADQUARTERS*. I HAVE A *MESSAGE*... A MESSAGE FOR THE *WORLD!*〉

〈OUR ONLY HOPE LIES WITH THE *BEINGS* IN THOSE SHIPS ABOVE.〉

〈THEY ARE OUR *BENEFACTORS*, HERE TO HELP US! DO YOU *UNDERSTAND*, FRIEND?〉

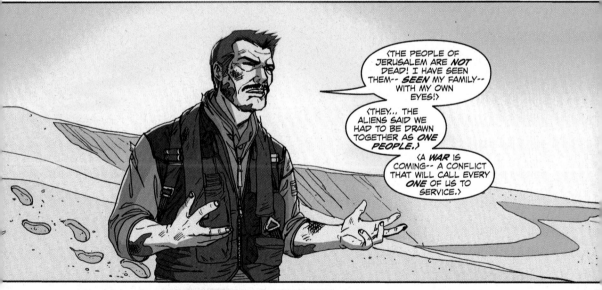

〈THE PEOPLE OF JERUSALEM ARE *NOT* DEAD! I HAVE SEEN THEM-- *SEEN* MY FAMILY-- WITH MY OWN EYES!〉

〈THEY... THE ALIENS SAID WE HAD TO BE DRAWN TOGETHER AS *ONE PEOPLE*.〉

〈A *WAR* IS COMING-- A CONFLICT THAT WILL CALL EVERY *ONE* OF US TO SERVICE.〉

〈WE HAVE BEEN *DRAFTED*-- EVERY MAN, WOMAN AND CHILD ON *EARTH*.〉

〈AND IF WE WISH TO SAVE OUR PLANET, WE WILL FIGHT TO THE *DEATH!*〉

CHAPTER THREE
THE LAST SHALL BE FIRST

MY NAME IS *COLONEL GIORA SHALIACH*, AND I HAVE A *MESSAGE* FOR ALL HUMANITY.

DAVID BEN-GURION ONCE SAID, *"IN ISRAEL, IN ORDER TO BE A REALIST YOU MUST BELIEVE IN MIRACLES".*

THE TIME HAS COME FOR US *ALL* TO BE REALISTS, AND TO BELIEVE IN MIRACLES.

THERE'S... THERE'S NO EASY WAY TO SAY THIS... TO MAKE IT SOUND SANE.

TO MAKE IT SOUND *FAIR*.

"WE HAVE BEEN DRAFTED INTO A CONFLICT THAT WILL DETERMINE NOT ONLY *OUR* FATE, BUT THAT OF *HUNDREDS* OF WORLDS.

"*EVERY* ONE OF US WILL BE CALLED TO SERVE.

"THOSE UNABLE TO *FIGHT* WILL BE ASSIGNED ROLES THAT... THAT ARE *APPROPRIATE* TO THEIR AGE OR CONDITION.

"*BORDERS* NO LONGER MATTER. RACE, CREED, STATUS... *NONE* OF THAT MATTERS ANYMORE.

"OUR *OLD* LIVES ARE GONE FOREVER."

"BUT THESE BEINGS-- THESE *BENEFACTORS*-- HAVE GIVEN US *MIRACLES.*

"THEY'VE CURED *CANCER.*

"AND MY FAMILY-- THE PEOPLE OF JERUSALEM-- ARE *ALIVE!*

"THE CITY ITSELF WAS SACRIFICED-- TO BRING US *TOGETHER...* TO UNITE US AS A *RACE.* I PRAY IT HAS SUCCEEDED...

"...BECAUSE THEY *SHOWED* ME THINGS. THINGS THAT MADE ME *WEEP* IN FEAR AND REVULSION.

"I... I HAVE SEEN THE *ENEMY."*

THE END IS HERE.

I KNOW YOU ARE AFRAID... THAT MANY HAVE BEGUN TO *DISAPPEAR.*

YOU FEAR THEY ARE DEAD-- THEY ARE *NOT.* THEY HAVE BEEN *DRAFTED.*

I *IMPLORE* YOU... DO NOT *RESIST.* WE HAVE ONLY MONTHS BEFORE OUR *TRUE* ADVERSARY ARRIVES...

"...AND UNITY IS OUR ONLY HOPE OF SURVIVAL."

RRMFF

RRMFF

STOP IT! GET **OUT** OF HERE!

THIS IS MY **SISTER'S** ROOM!

EASY KID...

PRESTON WALKER! WHAT IN HEAVEN'S NAME ARE YOU **DOING?**

ROBIN'S FUNERAL WAS YESTERDAY. WE LAID HER TO **REST.** NOW, WE MOVE ON.

THIS IS **LIFE,** SON. IF YOU CAN'T DEAL WITH IT--

"--HOW WILL YOU EVER BECOME A **LEADER?**"

IT'S **HIM...** HIM. IT'S **REALLY** HIM. PRESIDENT WALKER...!

PRESIDENT **WANKER** IS MORE LIKE IT.

WH-WHO **ARE** YOU PEOPLE? WHERE AM I... AND WHERE'S MY WIFE?

I WOULD PRESUME YOUR WIFE IS BACK IN WASHINGTON. AS TO WHERE **WE** ARE...? CAN'T HELP YOU WITH **THAT** ONE, LUV.

IN OTHER WORDS, **WE'RE** JUST AS LOST AS **YOU** ARE... UH, PRESTON.

LAST THING **I** REMEMBER IS GETTING READY TO DO A BBC SEGMENT IN LONDON.

OH, I'D SAY HE'S **MUCH** MORE LOST THAN WE ARE.

YOU'RE IRISH... SHE'S ENGLISH? WHAT THE HELL **IS** THIS?

MY GUESS? WE'RE ON OUR WAY TO BEING ABSORBED INTO THE ALIEN'S ARMY. NOT THAT I PLAN ON GOING **EASY**, MIND YOU.

GUESS WE HAVE THAT MUCH IN COMMON, EH, MR. EX-PRESIDENT?

WHAT'S **THAT** SUPPOSED TO MEAN? I'M **STILL**--

UM, EVERYONE...?

THAT **OTHER** GUY'S AWAKE.

WASHINGTON, D.C.

WHERE THE FUCK IS MY *HUSBAND*, STEPHAN?!

AND HOW DID WE NOT SEE THESE THINGS *COMING*? I MEAN, NASA? NORAD?

YOU'D THINK WITH BILLION DOLLAR BUDGETS, THEY'D BE ABLE TO WARN US ABOUT A GODDAMN *ALIEN INVASION!*

MRS. WALKER... LOOK, I'M *SORRY.* I DON'T KNOW *WHERE* THE PRESIDENT IS. I DON'T KNOW *WHY* WE COULDN'T SEE THEM COMING.

OH, STEPHAN... WHY IS ALL THIS *HAPPENING*? W-WHAT ARE WE GOING TO *DO*?

I DON'T *KNOW*, LORI.

I DON'T KNOW.

WISH I COULD SAY THE MILITARY COULD DO SOMETHING...

...BUT WE WOULDN'T EVEN KNOW WHERE TO BEGIN *LOOKING* FOR A WEAKNESS.

AND EVEN IF WE DID, HOW WOULD WE *EXPLOIT* IT? CHRIST, THEY ANNIHILATED JERUSALEM AND CURED CANCER IN THE SAME DAY--

--THEIR TECHNOLOGY MUST BE *CENTURIES* AHEAD OF OURS!

M-MAYBE WE CAN SEND A *DELEGATION* TO THEM--

"DELEGATION"? HE'S BEEN *DRAFTED*, LORI.

YOU HEARD SHALIACH'S MESSAGE-- IT'S ONLY A MATTER OF TIME BEFORE THEY TAKE *US*, TOO.

TO THESE ALIENS... WE'RE ALL THE *SAME.*

W-WHERE...?

YOU SPEAK ENGLISH... THAT'S *GOOD*. LET'S HOPE THE *OTHER* FELLOW DOES, TOO.

ARE YOU OKAY?

I-I *THINK* SO. I WAS HOME... IN JERSEY CITY. WHERE AM I *NOW*?

AND NOT TO BE RUDE, BUT WHO ARE *YOU*?

RABBI SRUELIK MENDELSOHN. I'M PLEASED TO MEET YOU, THOUGH I'D HAVE PREFERRED IT TO BE UNDER *SANER* CIRCUMSTANCES.

MY NAME IS *SADIQ AL-ASMARI*... I AM AN *IMAM*.

INTERESTING. LET'S TEND TO OUR FRIEND...

¿NGH¿ ¿DONDE ESTAN...?

I SPEAK SEVERAL LANGUAGES, BUT SPANISH, I REGRET, IS NOT *ONE* OF THEM.

'S OKAY... I SPEAK ENGLISH. I'M ERNESTO... *FATHER ERNESTO CARDENAL.*

A RABBI, AN IMAM AND A PRIEST... SOUNDS LIKE THE BEGINNING OF A BAD *JOKE.*

FWISSHH

MEN OF FAITH--

CHAS VCHOLILE...!

CHOSEN...? CHOSEN FOR *WHAT*?

YOU ARE PEACEMAKERS. *WE* ARE EMISSARIES OF PEACE AS WELL, *PERSECUTED* ACROSS THE COSMOS.

DESPERATION HAS DRIVEN US HERE... DESPERATION BORN OF *THE GREAT EVIL*.

WE'VE STUDIED YOUR WORLD FOR SO VERY, VERY LONG. DO YOU KNOW HOW IT *PAINS* US TO IMPERIL THIS BLUE ORB...?

KNOWING THAT IT INSPIRED EVERY DREAM, EVERY IDEA, EVERY *BELIEF* YOUR RACE EVER HAD?

IMAGINE HOW *WE* FEEL. WHAT EXACTLY DO YOU WANT FROM *US*...?

YOUR VOICES ARE STRONG, *SINCERE*.

IF OUR TWO SPECIES ARE TO WEATHER THE COMING STORM, THERE MUST BE *COMMUNION*.

MY GOD! THE FLOOR--! W-WE'RE ON ONE OF THEIR

PLEASE. WE ASK THAT YOU *RAISE* YOUR VOICES AS NEVER BEFORE... *ALLAY* THE FEARS AND ANGUISH OF YOUR BRETHREN.

WH-WHERE THE HELL *AM* I? WHO *ARE* YOU PEOPLE?

WHERE'S MY *SISTER*... MY MOTHER?

EASY THERE, PAL... EASY. I'M *KRIS*.

AS YOU CAN TELL FROM MY, UH, ATTIRE, I GOT SNATCHE' WITHOUT ANY *WARNIN'* SAME AS YOU--

LET *ME* HANDLE THIS. SON, I'M *PRESIDENT PRESTON WALKER.*

ARE YOU *SHITTING* ME...?

NO WORRIES, FRIEND... BEFORE LONG HE'LL REALIZE PRESIDENTS AND SUCH ARE A THING O' THE *PAST.*

JESUS...!

YOU REALLY *ARE* THE PRESIDENT...!

WAS THE PRESIDENT. AS FOR THE REST OF US...

NAME'S O'KAINE. *LUCAS O'KAINE.*

KRIS NELSON, FROM ST. LOUIS.

AUDREY... *AUDREY MARTIN.* UM, FROM VANCOUVER.

MY NAME IS *DEVON MCNEIL.* AND *YOU* ARE...?

GABRIEL CONTRERAS. FROM NEW YORK.

WHO'S *THAT* BACK THERE...?

SHE'S SOME KIND OF *ARAB.* HASN'T UTTERED A WORD *YET.*

THERE'S NO NEED FOR THE *ATTITUDE,* WALKER. NOT TO MENTION THE *IGNORANCE.*

WE'RE OBVIOUSLY FROM ALL OVER THE *WORLD.* MAYBE SHE DOESN'T SPEAK--

I SPEAK *ENGLISH* PERFECTLY WELL. I WAS MERELY TAKING THE MEASURE OF MY FELLOW *PAWNS.*

I AM *RAISA.*

"PAWNS"? WHAT DO *YOU* KNOW ABOUT ALL THIS?

IS IT NOT *OBVIOUS?* I HATE YOUR FREEDOMS. THIS IS ALL AN ELABORATE *TERRORIST* PLOT--

WHOA, WHOA, WHOA. MR. PRESIDENT... RAISA.

WE'RE OBVIOUSLY ALL IN THE SAME *BOAT* HERE. *SNIPING* AT EACH OTHER'S NOT GOING TO HELP.

IF WE WANT TO GET BACK TO OUR FAMILIES, WE'RE GOING TO NEED TO KEEP OUR SHIT TOGETHER AND THINK *RATIONALLY.*

THE BOY SPEAKS WITH *WISDOM.*

LUCAS O'KAINE. WE'D HOPED WE COULD HARNESS THE AGGRESSIVE NATURE YOU INHERITED FROM YOUR *FATHER*--

M-MY *DA?* HOW DO YOU MONSTERS KNOW SO MUCH ABOUT US?!

LUCAS! FOR GOD'S SAKE MAN, PUT THE GUN *DOWN!*

BE DOG WIDE, PONCHO. THIS IS BETWEEN ME AN' THIS THING!

HEED HIS WORDS, LUCAS O'KAINE.

AIMED AT ME, YOUR ANGER IS IMPOTENT. MAKE IT THE WEAPON YOU TRAIN ON THE ENEMY--

RAHHHH!

BLAM! BLAM! BLAM!

FSH

FSH FSH

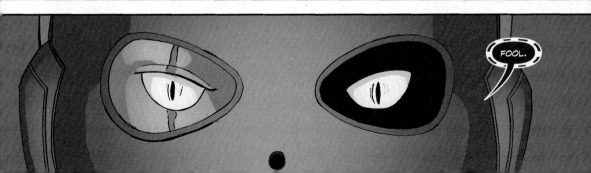

FOOL.

≈NRRGGHHH≈

VOIP!

JESUS—!

OHGOD OHGOD OHGOD

YOU TAKE US FROM OUR FAMILIES... NOW YOU *MURDER* ONE OF US?

HOW CAN YOU EXPECT US TO *FOLLOW* YOU?

DO YOU NOT YET *UNDERSTAND?* YOU HAVE NO CHOICE.

COME WITH ME...

...AND *SALVATION* MAY YET BELONG TO US ALL.

HEY...! WAIT. *WAIT!*

I-I'M *NOT* TAKING ANOTHER STEP 'TIL I KNOW WHAT'S HAPPENED TO MY SISTER AND MOTHER!

AND MY *WIFE.* I NEED TO KNOW... IS SHE OKAY?

SEVERAL YOUNG WOMEN *DEPEND* ON ME... THEY COULD BE IN GRAVE *DANGER* ALONE.

YOUR *SPECIES* TEETERS ON THE BRINK OF ANNIHILATION, YET YOU AGONIZE OVER THE FATE OF *INDIVIDUALS?*

VERY WELL.

LUCIA AND LOURDES REMAIN *SAFE* IN YOUR FAMILY'S DWELLING, GABRIEL CONTRERAS.

PRESTON WALKER. YOUR *LIFE-MATE* LORI, THOUGH ALARMED OVER YOUR *DISAPPEARANCE,* IS SECURE.

RAISA. SOHILA, ARYANA, AND HASEENA HAVE FOUND REFUGE WITH A GROUP OF BEDOUIN.

KRISTOFER NELSON. YOUR PARENTS ARE SAFE AND *UNCONCERNED* AS TO YOUR *WHEREABOUTS.*

DEVON MCNEIL. YOUR *EX-HUSBAND* IS WELL.

AUDREY MARTIN--

NO NEED FOR THE UPDATE, UGLY. I DON'T *HAVE* ANY FAMILY.

INDEED. NOW, *FOLLOW* ME THROUGH THE FINAL GATEWAY...

MY GOD... THERE MUST BE THOUSANDS OF PEOPLE HERE!

MOVE! YOU WILL WITNESS FAR *GREATER* SIGHTS IN THE MONTHS TO COME!

P-PRESIDENT *WALKER!* THANK GOD! YOU HAVE TO *DO* SOMETHING!

IT'S *ME*-- PHIL BRISTOL! PLEASE, STOP THEM... TELL THEM THEY CAN'T TAKE PEOPLE LIKE *US!*

FOR GOD'S SAKE, I'M A *WRITER!*

BRISTOL...? I--

YOUR PECULIAR SOCIAL CUSTOMS, WHICH BESTOWED POWER ON THIS MAN, *BAFFLE* ME.

BUT LOOK TO HIM NO MORE. HE IS A *SOLDIER* NOW. AS ARE *YOU.*

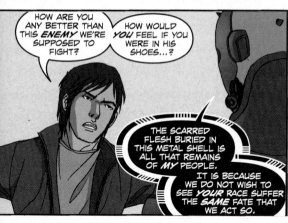

HOW ARE YOU ANY BETTER THAN THIS *ENEMY* WE'RE SUPPOSED TO FIGHT?

HOW WOULD *YOU* FEEL IF YOU WERE IN HIS SHOES...?

THE SCARRED FLESH BURIED IN THIS METAL SHELL IS ALL THAT REMAINS OF *MY* PEOPLE.

IT IS BECAUSE WE DO NOT WISH TO SEE *YOUR* RACE SUFFER THE *SAME* FATE THAT WE ACT SO.

I-I CAN'T. I C-CAN'T *DO* THIS...

AUDREY?

§SHHH§ YOU'RE GOING TO BE OKAY. WE'RE GOING TO TAKE CARE OF EACH OTHER...

THIS SHOW IS ALL VERY *INTENTIONAL.* THEY *WANT* US OFF OUR BEARINGS. TO MAKE US *COMPLIANT.*

DON'T GIVE THEM THE *SATISFACTION.*

VERY *INSIGHTFUL,* DEVON MCNEIL. CLEARLY, YOUR WARTIME *EXPERIENCE* WILL SERVE YOU WELL.

ONE CAN HARDLY BLAME YOU FOR SEEKING *REFUGE* FROM REALITY, GIVEN ITS CURRENT STATE--

‹W-WHA...?›

--NEVERTHELESS, *THIS* IS SOMETHING YOU DO NOT NEED.

THIS IS *MADNESS.* DO WE EVEN KNOW WHERE WE *ARE...?*

I'M FAIRLY CERTAIN WE'RE IN *JAKARTA...* I DID MISSIONARY WORK HERE ONCE.

SRUELIK... WHY *US?* AND ARE WE EVEN BUYING INTO THIS... THIS *MISSION?*

THEY'RE PUSHING OUR BUTTONS, *THAT* MUCH IS CLEAR. WHETHER IT IMPLIES *MALICE* IS NOT.

I DON'T *CARE* WHAT MOTIVATES THESE BEINGS. THEY COULD BE ANGELS OR DEMONS, IT DOESN'T *MATTER.*

THE COMMON THREADS THAT BIND US ALL *STILL* BIND US.

AND NOW, MORE THAN EVER, PEOPLE NEED TO BE *REMINDED* OF THAT.

‹WHAT HAVE WE DONE TO DESERVE THIS...?› *

* TRANSLATED FROM THE GERMAN. --MIKE

YAHHHHH!

‹WHAT THE HELL *IS* IT-?›

‹GET *AWAY* FROM IT! GET *AWAY* FROM IT!›

‹WH-WHAT'S *HAPPENING?* WHAT DID YOU *SEE...?*›

‹MOVE! LET ME *OUT!*›

‹*WHAT?* WHAT *IS* IT?›

‹I THINK... I THINK WE SAW WHAT *CAUSED* THE EARTHQUAKE!›

‹ARE YOU *MAD!?* YOU HAVE NO *IDEA* WHAT'S DOWN THERE!›

‹IF WHAT CAUSED ALL THIS DEATH AND DESTRUCTION IS BELOW, I'LL BE DAMNED IF I'M NOT GOING TO *PISS* ON IT!›

WOODSIDE, NEW YORK

EXCUSE ME...!
PLEASE, I'M TRYING TO FIND MY *BROTHER*...

GABRIEL... PLEASE, GABRIEL BE AT THE STORE...

NO.

COMEL
WIDES

OPEN

OH, G-GABRIEL...

WHERE *ARE* YOU...?

SOLDIERS MUST LEARN TO FEND FOR *THEMSELVES.* NOW...

...ENTER THE *GATEWAY.* LET US BEGIN YOUR TRAINING.

FROM THIS MOMENT ON, EVERY PIECE OF EQUIPMENT YOU USE WILL BE OF OUR HOSTS' MANUFACTURE...

...AND ALL OF IT IS BASED UPON THEIR OWN NATURE, WHICH IS PSIONIC. IT IS CRUCIAL YOU *REMEMBER* THIS.

"PSIONIC"...?

GUIDED BY THE *MIND.*

WE'RE TIRED. AND *STARVING.* AREN'T WE GOING TO BE *FED...?*

HELL, THESE GUYS CURED MY *CANCER.*

I'LL WALK THROUGH ANY DOOR THEY *WANT* ME TO.

CAN'T LET HIM GO IT *ALONE,* CAN WE...?

CANCER...?

DO I *HAVE* TO...?

MANY SEE YOU AS A COWARD AND A WEAKLING. AND PERHAPS, IN YOUR DEEPEST THOUGHTS, YOU VIEW *YOURSELF* THIS WAY AS WELL.

BUT PIERCE THIS VEIL, AND YOU MAY RETURN WITH A *DIFFERENT* KNOWLEDGE.

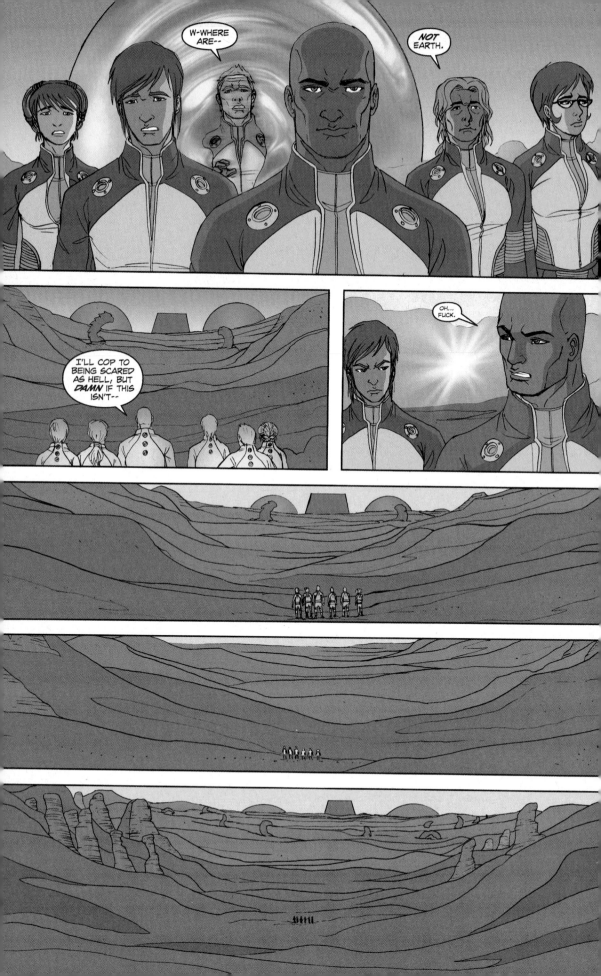

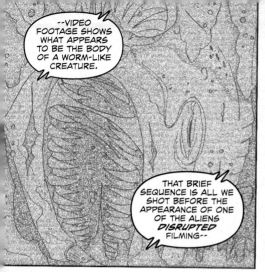

--VIDEO FOOTAGE SHOWS WHAT APPEARS TO BE THE BODY OF A WORM-LIKE CREATURE.

THAT BRIEF SEQUENCE IS ALL WE SHOT BEFORE THE APPEARANCE OF ONE OF THE ALIENS *DISRUPTED* FILMING--

WOODSIDE, N.Y.

--BUT THOSE *SEVEN SECONDS* OF BLURRY VIDEO COULD SHATTER ANY ILLUSIONS WE MAY STILL HAVE REGARDING THE *CONFLICT* THAT LOOMS OVER US.

BECAUSE IF THIS CREATURE *CAUSED* THE EARTHQUAKE IN BERLIN, WHICH AT LEAST *SEEMS* LIKELY--

--WE HAVE TO ASK, HOW MANY *OTHERS* ARE ALREADY HERE?

ARE THESE MONSTROSITIES EATING AWAY AT THE GROUND BENEATH OUR FEET AT THIS VERY MOMENT?

MAMA?

GABRIEL'S NOT VOLUNTEERING AT THE CHURCH, *IS* HE?

HE'S BEEN *TAKEN*... DRAFTED BY THOSE THINGS.

... I-I'M S-S-SORRY FOR LYING...

I J-JUST DIDN'T WANT TO *SCARE* YOU.

LUCIA! WHAT HAPPENED TO YOU!?

I... I WAS *ATTACKED*

I WENT LOOKING FOR GABRIEL... HOPING FOR A *MIRACLE.*

IT'S *INSANE* OUT THERE, MAMA... LOOTING, PEOPLE JUST... TRYING TO *TAKE* WHAT THEY W-W-WANT!

AND I'M AFRAID WE'RE NEVER GOING TO *SEE* GABRIEL EVER AGAIN.

SHHH. YOUR FATHER WILL WATCH OVER HIM. NO MATTER *WHERE* HE IS...

SEE THAT *STRUCTURE* IN THE DISTANCE?

THAT THING... THAT *MONOLITH*... IS THE *ONLY* THING HERE THAT LOOKS... *CONSTRUCTED.* NOT NATURAL. IT'S *GOT* TO BE WHERE WE'RE SUPPOSED TO GO.

I'D SAY THAT'S A GOOD ASSESSMENT, GABRIEL.

GUYS...?

I DON'T THINK WE SHOULD GO *ANYWHERE.*

THIS IS SUPPOSED TO BE SOME SORT OF *TRAINING*... WHY WOULD THEY JUST *LEAVE* US HERE TO OUR OWN DEVICES?

SHE'S *RIGHT.* THEY WOULDN'T HAVE SENT US A BILLION MILES FROM HOME JUST TO *ABANDON* US.

FUCKING BULLSHIT...

WHAT'S *YOUR* PROBLEM, WALKER?

I *SAID,* IT'S FUCKING *BULLSHIT!* LETTING THAT WOMAN SCOUT AHEAD.

SHE'S PROBABLY SPENT THE LAST FIVE YEARS MAKING *BOMBS* AND LEAVING THEM BY ROADSIDES--

OH, CUT THE CRAP, YOU--

KRIS-- *MR. PRESIDENT*... YOU BOTH NEED TO TAKE IT *DOWN* A NOTCH.

RAISA SPENT HER WHOLE LIFE IN AFGHANISTAN... DESERT TERRAIN LIKE *THIS* IS HER ELEMENT.

HE'S *RIGHT.* AND *THAT'S* WHY WE'VE BEEN LEFT HERE-- TO FORCE US TO BOND AS A *TEAM.*

IF WE WANT TO GET HOME, WE NEED TO TAKE ADVANTAGE OF EACH OTHER'S *SKILLS.*

I'M GLAD TO HEAR YOU *SAY* THAT, DR. MCNEIL, BECAUSE I'VE *FOUND* SOMETHING...

...THIS PLACE IS NOT SO *ALIEN* AFTER ALL.

SHIT.

"SHIT" WHAT?

THIS MEANS THERE'S GOING TO BE SOMEONE TO *SHOOT* AT.

I CAN DEAL WITH THAT.

ALWAYS *HATED* GUNS... SEEN TOO MANY VICTIMS *FIRSTHAND*.

STUCK MY FINGERS INTO GAPING BULLET WOUNDS TRYING TO STOP THE BLEEDING...

FUCK IT.

THEY *CURED* ME. THEY WANT ME TO FIGHT, I'LL *FIGHT*.

THERE'S NO *TRIGGER*.

YOU *NOTICED*. THESE CREATURES ARE *TOYING* WITH US!

I DON'T THINK SO.

REMEMBER WHAT... WHAT HANNIBAL SAID ABOUT THE ALIENS' TECHNOLOGY? HOW IT WORKS?

LET ME TRY SOMETHING...

I DON'T GET IT... WHAT'S SHE--

SHOOOM!

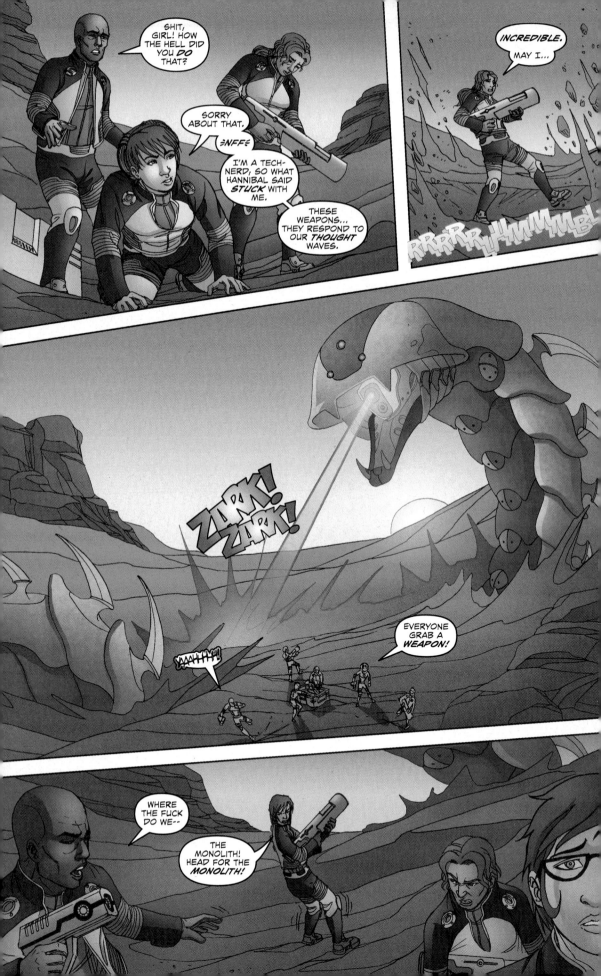

...NO MATTER WHERE WE ARE ON THIS WORLD AT THIS MOMENT, WE LOOK UP AND SEE THE SAME *NIGHTMARE* LOOMING OVERHEAD.

IF *THAT* DOESN'T AWAKEN US TO WHAT HAS ALWAYS BEEN TRUE-- TO ALL THAT WE SHARE-- *NOTHING* WILL.

LOOK AT *US:* CHRISTIAN, JEW, AND MUSLIM. OUR PEOPLES HAVE SPILLED EACH OTHER'S BLOOD AT THE SLIGHTEST PROVOCATION-- OR WITHOUT ANY AT *ALL.*

AND YET, EACH GROUP IS MERELY EXPRESSING *VARIATIONS* ON THE SAME SPIRITUAL TRADITION... ...WE ARE ALL *SONS OF ABRAHAM.*

WE ARE HERE TO PROVIDE AN *EXAMPLE,* TO URGE YOU TO OVERCOME FEAR, TO HOLD FAST TO--

UNGH!

HO THREW THAT STONE? WHAT *COWARD* STRIKES FROM THE ANONYMITY OF A *CROWD?*

SHUT YOUR *MOUTH,* JEW! *ALL* OF YOU SHUT YOUR MOUTHS!

HOW *DARE* YOU LECTURE US WITH THESE MINDLESS *PLATITUDES?*

YOU KNOW WHAT THOSE SHIPS ABOVE HAVE PROVEN? THAT WE'RE JUST ANOTHER RACE OF *ANIMALS.* THE IDEA OF THE COMMON GOOD IS A *JOKE.* A *COSMIC* JOKE.

EVERYTHING THAT MADE THE WORLD WORK HAS COME TO A HALT. VERY SOON, THE MOST *BASIC* NECESSITIES OF LIFE WILL BE IN SHORT SUPPLY...

JAK MANIA

...SO DON'T TALK TO US ABOUT THE *COMMON* GOOD. THE COMMON GOOD WILL GET US *KILLED.*

HELP!
HEELLLLP!

STAY *AWAY* FROM HER, YOU BASTARDS!

AUDREY, TAKE *COVER!* BEHIND THOSE *ROCKS!*

SHOOM!!
SHOOM!!

≥HFF≥
≥HFF≥

AUDREY...

WH-WHO...?

AUUUDREY...

HERE, AUDREY...

N-NO... IT'S NOT POSSIBLE!

ALIYA...?

SIS!

ALIYA... THIS CAN'T BE *REAL*... HOW IS THIS *HAPPENING?*

HEY, THERE'S *ENOUGH* DRAMA IN THIS PLACE. DON'T *YOU* LOSE IT ON ME.

GOD, AM I GLAD TO SEE A FRIENDLY FACE. TELL ME *EVERYTHING* YOU'RE UP TO NOW!

ALIYA... ALIYA, I'VE MISSED YOU SO *MUCH!*

HEY... SHHHH. ONLY ANOTHER SIX *MONTHS* AND I'M OUT!

YOU SHOULDN'T *BE* HERE... IT SHOULD HAVE BEEN ME.

IT SHOULD HAVE BEEN *ME!*

SHHHH! THEY *LISTEN* TO OUR CONVERSATIONS!

YOU HAVE A CHANCE TO *MAKE* SOMETHING OF YOURSELF. IT'S WHAT MOM AND DAD WOULD HAVE *WANTED*.

I'LL BE OUT IN SIX MONTHS, NO PROBLEM. IT'S NOT SO BAD IN HERE.

THERE ARE A FEW *TROUBLE-MAKERS* I NEED TO STEER CLEAR OF, BUT THAT'S ABOUT IT.

TIME'S *UP*, MARTIN.

NOOO! ALIYA, *PLEASE!*

CHILL, AUD'..., I'LL SEE YOU NEXT WEEK.

NO YOU *WON'T!* IT WAS *ME! I* DID IT! I SHOULD BE IN HERE!

THIS IS WHAT I ACCEPTED, AUDREY. THIS IS WHAT I *CHOSE*, BECAUSE I *LOVE* YOU.

NOW *WALK* OUT THAT DOOR. WITHOUT A SECOND *LOOK*. LIVE YOUR LIFE...

...*PROMISE* ME, NO MATTER WHAT, YOU'LL LIVE YOUR LIFE!

AUDREY!

R-RAISA? DEVON?

QUICKLY, GIRL. HAVE YOU NOT NOTICED... THESE HILLS *AREN'T* HILLS?

ZKN! ZARK!

SOON...

GOTTA GET *AWAY* FROM *THOSE* THINGS...

BETTER OFF ON MY ≥HFF≥ OWN...

W-WHAT...?

HOW THE...? *WHERE AM* I!?

YOU'RE EXACTLY WHERE YOU *NEED* TO BE, PAL.

BUT WHAT *IS* THIS? THEY BROUGHT *YOU* HERE, TOO?

SIT DOWN... YOU LOOK LIKE YOU'VE BEEN THROUGH *HELL.*

YEAH. YEAH, I HAVE.

I'M SO *TIRED...* SO FUCKING TIRED OF EVERY- THING.

THIS'LL SETTLE YOU DOWN, BRO. I CAN TELL YOU *WANT* IT.

I... I *CAN'T*. I DON'T *DRINK* ANYMORE...

AHH, IT'S JUST *ONE* DRINK. IT'S THE END OF THE WORLD AS WE KNOW IT. WHAT'S THE *HARM?*

MAN LIKE *YOU* NEEDS HIS WITS ABOUT HIM. THIS'LL TAKE THE *EDGE* OFF--

I SAID *NO!*

KRASSH!

WHY? WHY NOT JUST GIVE IN JUST THIS *ONCE?*

BECAUSE... BECAUSE GETTING *SOBER'S* THE ONLY THING I EVER DID FOR *MYSELF.*

THE ONLY THING THAT SOMEONE ELSE COULDN'T DO FOR ME.

STRONG ENOUGH TO FACE REALITY ON YOUR OWN, EH?

SUIT YOUR SELF...

HEY! YOU GUYS *HFF* OKAY...?

KRIS! THANK GOD! *WE'RE* OKAY. ARE *YOU*...?

ASIDE FROM MAKING A COMPLETE DICK OF MYSELF TO WALKER? JUST *FINE*.

HAVE YOU GUYS *SEEN* HIM?

I'M SORRY, KRIS... BUT NO. WE *HAVEN'T*.

OH, *SHIT!* I SAID SOMETHING *STUPID* AND HE RAN OFF... CHRIST, HE COULD BE *DEAD* NOW!

WE'LL *FIND* HIM. TAKE IT EASY...

WE NEED TO FIND SHELTER. IT'S SUNSET, AND WE DON'T KNOW *NEARLY* ENOUGH ABOUT THIS LAND TO TRY CROSSING IT AT NIGHT.

SHELTER? WHERE ARE WE GOING TO FIND *THAT?*

RIGHT *HERE*. IT'S AS *CLOSE* AS WE'RE GOING TO GET TO SAFETY. AT LEAST WE HAVE A MEASURE OF *COVER* FROM THOSE... THINGS.

YOU THINK THEY'RE DOING THIS TO *EVERY-ONE?*

WHAT DO YOU MEAN?

ALL THOSE *PEOPLE* WE SAW BACK ON THE SHIP. DO YOU THINK THE ALIENS HAVE SENT ALL OF *THEM* ONTO... ONTO...

HEH HEH.

DID I *MISS* SOMETHING? WHAT'S SO BLOODY *AMUSING?*

I'M SORRY. IT'S JUST... EVERY FIVE SECONDS I CATCH MYSELF THINKING, "THIS CAN'T BE *REAL*".

BUT IT *IS.*

YOU SEEM TO HAVE BOUGHT *INTO* ALL OF THIS. *WHY?*

YEAH... WHAT GOOD'S BEING CURED OF CANCER IF YOU END UP *DEAD* ANYWAY?

IT'S NOT *JUST* THE CANCER. THINK ABOUT IT... THE WHOLE *WORLD'S* BEEN GIVEN A NEW START. *NONE* OF US HAS TO BE WHO WE WERE BEFORE.

AND... LOOK, I'M A *PARAMEDIC.* MY WHOLE *LIFE'S* BEEN ABOUT HELPING PEOPLE, DOING SOMETHING WORTHWHILE. HAVING A *PURPOSE.*

WHAT'S MORE WORTHWHILE THAN SAVING OUR *PLANET?*

WISH *I* COULD BE SO BLISSFULLY NAIVE, LUV.

ME, I'M SCARED AS *HELL* TO BE SITTING HERE. AND THE FACT THAT THOSE CREATURES SEEM TO KNOW EVERYTHING *ABOUT* US...?

THAT SCARES ME EVEN *MORE.*

YAHH!

HUH!

JESUS...

≈HFF HFF≈

YOU... YOU OKAY?

OH, YEAH. *SWELL.*

LUCKY FOR ME I GOT A STRONG TICKER.

WELL... I DON'T KNOW ABOUT YOU, BUT I'M FREEZING MY *ASS* OFF.

I PASSED A BUNCH OF CAVES... MAYBE WE'D BE *WARMER* IN ONE OF THEM?

NO!

THAT IS... I THINK IT'D BE BETTER IF WE KEEP *MOVING.*

LET'S... JUST *WALK* FOR A WHILE.

SURE. NO PROBLEM.

SO. WHAT'S IT *FEEL* LIKE?

WHAT?

TO BE *PRESIDENT.*

FOR A WHILE, I THOUGHT IT WAS *FUN.*

WHEN I *FIRST* CAME TO OFFICE, THE WORLD WAS RELATIVELY PEACEFUL. BUT THEN... WELL, *YOU* KNOW.

PRETTY QUICK, I REALIZED *EVERY* DECISION I MADE WOULD AFFECT THE SAFETY OF *MILLIONS.*

I REALIZED EVERY POLICY HAD TO BE BASED ON RIGHT AND *WRONG,* NO MATTER WHAT.

NO COMPROMISES. NO *BARGAINING* WITH PEOPLE WHO'D JUST AS SOON SEE US DEAD.

THAT'S... *THAT'S* WHY I... WE... REJECTED THE ALIENS' OVERTURES.

ALL THOSE PEOPLE.

MR. PRESI- DENT...?

BECAUSE OF *ME.* BECAUSE OF ME, JERU- SALEM IS *GONE.*

THAT'S NOT YOUR *FAULT.* THE ALIENS--

I'M NOT LOOKING FOR YOUR FUCKIN' *PITY!*

OR YOUR FORGIVENESS. PEOPLE LIKE *YOU* HAVEN'T A GODDAMN *CLUE* WHAT IT'S LIKE TO BE *ME.*

WHO THE HELL WERE *THEY* TO TELL ME WHAT TO DO WITH MY COUNTRY? MY *PEOPLE?*

I'M THEIR *LEADER,* DAMMIT! THE PRESIDENT...

IT... IT'S MY DESTINY... MY PURPOSE. ISN'T IT...?

=YAWN=
YOU STAYED ON WATCH ALL **NIGHT?** YOU MUST BE--

I'M GOING TO HAVE TO TEACH ALL OF YOU TO BE MORE **QUIET** IN HOSTILE TERRITORY.

MMF!

MY **APOLO-GIES,** CHILD. THEY MADE OVER-HEAD PASSES THROUGHOUT THE NIGHT.

I-I THOUGHT WE'D **LOST** THEM...

OHHHH GOD... WHAT **IS** THIS PLACE? WHY ARE THEY **DOING** THIS TO US...?

WHAT I'VE SEEN HERE...

SHHHHH. BE STRONG, LITTLE ONE. WE'RE **ALL** TERRIFIED OF WHAT WE'VE SEEN HERE, BUT--

N-NO. YOU D-DON'T **UNDERSTAND.** I... I **SAW** SOME-THING. SOMETHING **IMPOSS-IBLE.**

YOU WILL TELL ME ALL ABOUT IT WHEN WE'VE REACHED **SAFETY.**

RIGHT NOW, WE NEED TO ROUSE THE OTHERS. OKAY?

OKAY.

SOON...

THERE'S THE **MONO-LITH.**

THESE SCULPTURES SHOULD PROVIDE SUFFICIENT COVER... AT LEAST ENOUGH TO GET US CLOSE.

WE'LL STICK TO THE LEFT SIDE OF THE VALLEY, CLOSE TO THE ROCKS.

HAVE YOUR **WEAPONS** READY AT ALL TIMES.

LET'S MOVE.

AREN'T YOU GOING TO... UM... TAKE **POINT?**

IT'S **BETTER** I COVER OUR REAR.

KRIS.

KEEP YOUR EYE ON THE OTHERS, ESPECIALLY AUDREY, WHEN THE **ATTACK** COMES...

...WE WILL COVER THEIR **ESCAPE.**

WHAT? WHY ARE WE *STOPPING?* DID YOU *SEE* SOMETHING...?

NO.

I NEED YOU TO *PROMISE* ME SOMETHING.

WHAT?

THAT YOU WON'T TELL THE OTHERS... HOW I *LOST* IT.

TELL THE *OTHERS...?* WE'VE GOT MORE *PRESSING* CONCERNS THAN TRADING GOSSIP.

BESIDES, WE'RE *ALL* LOSING IT. YOU WANT SOMETHING TO BE *ASHAMED* OF? WAIT TILL OUR OVERLORDS GET A LOOK AT MY *UNDERWEAR.*

HEH. MAKES *TWO* OF US, KID.

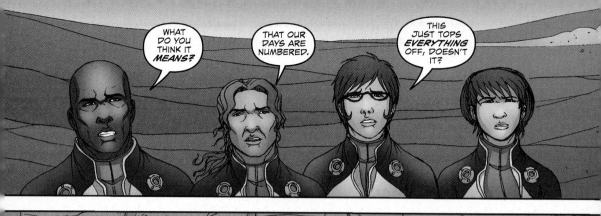

WHAT DO YOU THINK IT *MEANS?*

THAT OUR DAYS ARE NUMBERED.

THIS JUST TOPS *EVERYTHING* OFF, DOESN'T IT?

BASED UPON THE STORY THESE HIERO-GLYPHICS SEEM TO BE TELLING...

...I THINK IT'S SAFE TO ASSUME THOSE GIANT SCULPTURES DO INDEED REPRESENT THE ENEMY WE ARE MEANT TO *BATTLE.*

WASN'T THE POINT OF *REACHING* THIS THING TO GET HOME?

I DON'T SEE ANY--

JESUS! *THAT* ANSWER YOUR QUESTION?

FWOOSHH!

A LITTLE *TOO* DIRECTLY.

CHAPTER FIVE:
AS ABOVE, SO BELOW

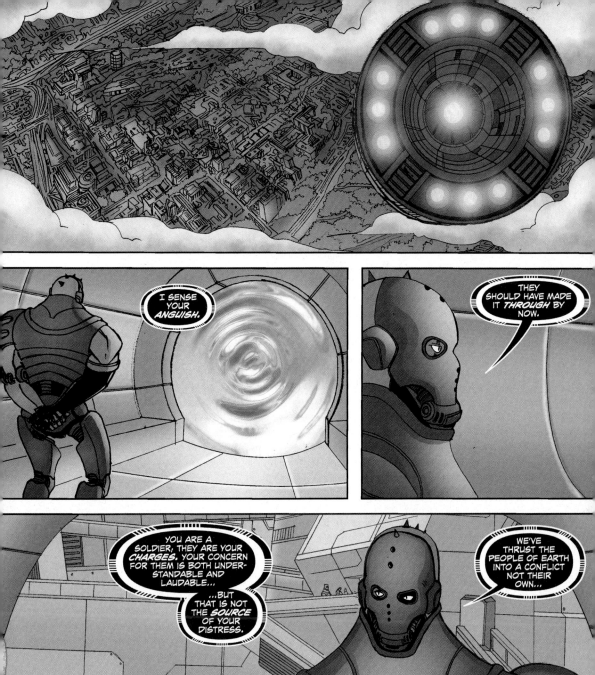

I SENSE YOUR *ANGUISH*.

THEY SHOULD HAVE MADE IT *THROUGH* BY NOW.

YOU ARE A SOLDIER, THEY ARE YOUR *CHARGES*. YOUR CONCERN FOR THEM IS BOTH UNDER-STANDABLE AND LAUDABLE...

...BUT THAT IS NOT THE *SOURCE* OF YOUR DISTRESS.

WE'VE THRUST THE PEOPLE OF EARTH INTO A CONFLICT NOT THEIR OWN...

...A WAR THAT WILL, IN ALL LIKELI-HOOD, RESULT IN THEIR *EXTINCTION*. BY WHAT *RIGHT* DO WE MAKE THESE DEMANDS OF THEM?

THE RIGHT THRUST UPON *US* TO STOP THE EVIL THAT DESTROYED *OUR* WORLDS.

...WHERE IS *GABRIEL CONTRERAS?*

OH, GOD, *NO!* GABRIEL!

C'MON, MAN, *C'MON!*

ZZZRT!

NO!!

WHAT THE *HELL?!*

OPEN THAT *PORTAL,* GODDAMN IT! WE CAN'T JUST *LEAVE* HIM THERE!

SEND *ME* BACK! I'LL GO *MYSELF--*

THERE IS NO *TIME* FOR THAT NOW.

FORGIVE ME, *ALL* OF YOU... BUT WE HAVE A FAR MORE *PRESSING* CONCERN. THE ENEMY...

THE ENEMY IS *HERE.*

HOLY SHIT! HOLY *SHIT!!*

KRAKOOM!

C-CAN'T STAY OUT IN THE *OPEN...*

WHAT THE...?

OH, *REAL* INVITING.

GUESS I DON'T HAVE MUCH OF A *CHOICE.*

HELLO?

WHAT THE HELL IS *THAT...?*

JESUS!

DON'T BE *AFRAID,* GABRIEL. I WON'T LET *ANYTHING* HURT YOU.

OH MY GOD...

DO YOU THINK IT'S AS BAD *EVERY-WHERE* AS IT IS HERE?

I HAVE NO IDEA, MAMA, BUT IF I HAD TO GUESS?

YES. I THINK IT'S *JUST* AS BAD EVERYWHERE ELSE IN THE WORLD.

HEY!

HEY, WHERE THE HELL ARE *YOU* TWO GOING?

DON'T LOOK, JUST IGNORE HIM...

IT'S *GONE*, DO YOU HEAR ME?

WHAT-EVER YOU'RE OUT HERE *LOOKING* FOR IS GONE!

POOR SOUL. HE'S *JUST* THE SORT WE NEED TO HELP.

WE CAN'T JUST SIT AROUND *WAITING* FOR GABRIEL TO COME BACK.

F-FATHER GONZALES...?

HE'S NOT *HERE*, MAMA...

...*NOBODY'S* HERE.

"NOBODY"?

OVER *HERE.*

SORRY TO STARTLE YOU.

I'M *LOURDES CONTRERAS,* AND THIS IS MY DAUGHTER *LUCIA.* MISTER...?

MICHAEL DALTON.

WHAT *ARE* YOU DOING HERE, MR. DALTON?

I JUST... IT PROBABLY SOUNDS *STUPID,* BUT I DIDN'T KNOW WHERE ELSE TO *GO.*

I MEAN, I'M NOT A *CHURCHGOER.* I'M NOT BIG ON THE *CLERGY* AND THEIR *DOGMA.*

BUT THE CHURCHES *THEMSELVES?* THEY'VE ALWAYS MADE ME FEEL... *SAFE.*

MR. DALTON, HAVE YOU SEEN FATHER GONZALES... THE PARISH PASTOR?

OR ANYONE *ELSE?*

PEOPLE HAVE BEEN IN AND OUT OF HERE ALL *NIGHT.* I'VE PROBABLY BEEN HERE FOR A GOOD TWELVE HOURS...

...BUT I HAVEN'T SEEN *ANY* PRIESTS.

WELL, WE'LL *FIND* HIM SOON ENOUGH.

IN THE MEANTIME... ARE YOU READY TO GET TO *WORK?*

YOU CALL THAT A **MEAL**?

HOOKING US UP TO SOME HR GIGER-LOOKING IV DRIP?

HEY... ISN'T THAT...?

SHALIACH?! THE ISRAELI PILOT THAT WAS KILLED?

THAT WAS A **DEMONSTRATION**, AS WAS THE RAZING OF JERUSALEM.

WE WOULD **NEVER** WANTONLY TAKE SO MANY INNOCENT LIVES. SHALIACH, AND JERUSALEM'S PEOPLE, **LIVE**.

YOU MEAN... YOU **LET** ME BELIEVE THEY WERE DEAD? THAT I'D GOTTEN MILLIONS OF PEOPLE **KILLED**?

WALKER... THEY'RE ALIVE, ISN'T THAT THE **IMPORTANT** PART?

ENOUGH. THE WORLD-EATERS ARE HERE. **THEY** CAUSED THE TREMORS THAT DEVASTATED YOUR CITIES.

ONE OF THEM YET **SURVIVES**. **WE** WILL HUNT IT DOWN.

YOU MEAN ONE OF THOSE **WORMS**? YOU BETTER BE ARMING US TO THE **TEETH**.

IT'S *ME*, GABRITO...

...IT'S *DADDY*.

NO...

SHHHH, SON. IT'S ME.

...NO YOU'RE *NOT*.

GET YOUR HANDS *OFF* ME.

GABRIEL? WHAT'S WRONG?

WHAT'S *WRONG?* WHAT'S *WRONG?!*

DO YOU THINK I'M *FUCKING* STUPID?

THIS IS ALL BULLSHIT. COMPLETE AND UTTER BULLSHIT.

YOU THINK I DON'T *GET* THAT THIS SOME SORT OF... *ILLUSION?*

YOU SICK BASTARDS. USING MY FATHER'S MEMORY...

SHOW ME WHAT YOU *REALLY* ARE.

SO BE IT.

I THINK I'M GONNA PUKE.

JOIN THE *CLUB.*

SAW THE NEWS REPORTS... BUT IT'S SO *DIFFERENT* FROM UP HERE... SO MUCH *WORSE.*

YOUR HEART RATES ARE *SPIKING...*

OTTAWA

...*CALM* YOURSELVES.

THERE, DO YOU SEE IT? THE EARTHEN WAKE OF A WORLD-EATER.

NOW. LET ME SHOW YOU HOW TO *KILL.*

WASHINGTON, D.C.

MRS. WALKER?

YOU *STARTLED* ME, AGENT FAAS. I DIDN'T REALIZE THERE WERE STILL ANY SECRET SERVICE *LEFT* HERE...

MY JOB IS TO *PROTECT* YOU. I'M GOING TO KEEP *DOING* IT UNTIL THEY TAKE ONE OR BOTH OF US.

ANYWAY... I THINK THERE'S SOMETHING YOU SHOULD *SEE* OUTSIDE.

OUTSIDE? IS EVERYTHING *OKAY...*?

WHEN... WHEN DID THIS *START*?

NOTICED THE FIRST A FEW HOURS A IT'S LIKE THE DON'T KNOW WHERE ELS TO *GO*.

BUT... I DON'T UNDERSTAND. WHAT DO THEY *WANT*?

THEY'RE DESPERATE FOR SOME- ONE TO TELL THEM WHAT TO DO, FOR A LEADER.

YOU'RE ABOUT THE CLOSEST THING THEY HAVE TO A *PRESIDENT* NOW.

T-TEST? YOU'RE FUCKING WITH MY *MIND* T-TO *TEST* ME?

OUR SURVIVAL WILL DEPEND ON YOUR RACE'S ABILITY TO *OVERCOME* FEAR AND EMOTION. *YOUR* RESPONSE WAS IMPRESSIVE.

IF YOU THINK *THIS* IS AN IMPRESSIVE RESPONSE, WE'RE *ALL* IN A LOT OF TROUBLE.

THE TERROR YOU FEEL IS AN *INSTINCTUAL* REACTION TO THE PRESENCE OF A BEING FAR REMOVED FROM HUMAN EXPERIENCE. IT WILL PASS IN TIME.

YOU CAN *READ* MINDS? *THAT'S* HOW YOU KNOW SO MUCH ABOUT US?

READ YOUR MINDS? *NO.* WE MERELY SENSE THOSE THOUGHTS AND EMOTIONS CLOSEST TO THE *SURFACE.*

NOW, COME. ANSWERS LIE *ELSEWHERE.*

WHAT *NOW?* MORE SCREWING WITH MY *MIND?*

UNFORTUNATELY... *YES.*

BUT *THIS* TIME, THE ILLUSION WILL BE DRAWN FROM *OUR* MEMORIES, *OUR* EMOTIONS.

WHAT I WILL SHOW YOU BEYOND THIS CREST... WILL MAKE CLEAR WHAT IS AT *STAKE.*

LOOK. UNDERSTAND WHAT HAPPENED TO *OUR* WORLD...

STOP... MAKE IT *STOP*.

"*HAS* COME"?!

TWO ADVANCE SCOUTS... OR SO WE *BELIEVE*.

NO. YOU *MUST* UNDERSTAND WHAT CAME TO OUR WORLD, AND MANY OTHERS.

YOU MUST UNDERSTAND WHAT HAS COME TO *EARTH*.

BUT... YOUR RACE IS SO FAR *BEYOND* OURS. IF *YOU* COULDN'T STOP THEM... WHAT HOPE DO *WE* HAVE?

PERHAPS *NONE.*

WHAT DOES THAT MATTER TO YOU? YOU DO NOT FEAR DEATH...A PART OF YOU EVEN *CRAVES* IT.

THERE *IS* AN AFTERLIFE, YOU KNOW.

YOU *CAN* BE WITH YOUR FATHER. AVOID THE BLOODSHED, THE GUILT AND TERROR OF WAR.

DO YOU *WISH* THIS?

WHAT'S CLOSEST TO THE SURFACE OF MY MIND *NOW?*

"... YOUR SISTER. YOUR MOTHER.

YOU FEAR YOU WILL NEVER *SEE* THEM AGAIN... AND, TRAGICALLY, THAT FEAR WILL LIKELY PROVE *JUSTIFIED.*

BUT IF YOU CAN PUT *ASIDE* YOUR GRIEF AND ANXIETY...

...YOU WILL HAVE THE CHANCE TO SAVE *MILLIONS* OF LIVES.

DON'T *PANIC!*
REMEMBER WHAT WE
KNOW ABOUT THEIR
TECHNOLOGY.

FOCUS...

SHE'S *RIGHT...*
THESE SHIPS ARE
ATTUNED TO OUR
THOUGHTS.

COME
ON!

TRYIN'...

I-I THINK
WE'VE *LOST*
THE MEN,
AUDREY...?

DON'T
TALK, I'M
TRYING TO
CONCEN-
TRATE!

CROOO!

KRAK!

THERE!
I
DID IT!

SHRAK!

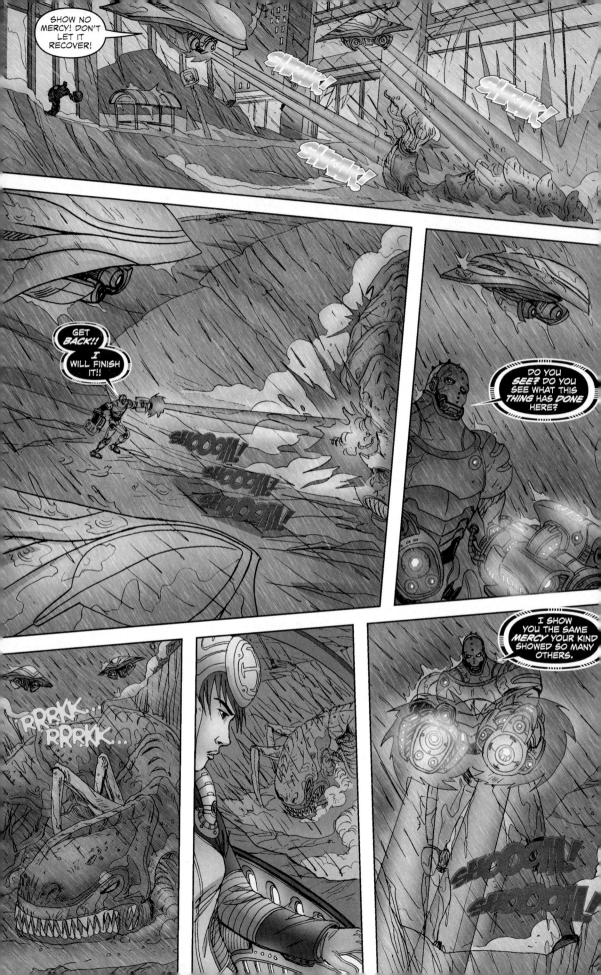

LOOK AT THIS! HOW COULD THINGS HAVE DETERIORATED SO *QUICKLY*?

WHY *WOULDN'T* THINGS BE DETERIORATING?

WHO'S DELIVERING THE *FOOD*? THE *GAS*? MEDICAL SUPPLIES?

FOR THAT MATTER, WHO'S *MANUFACTURING* THOSE THINGS? WHO'S *ADMINISTERING* THE CITY'S DAY-TO-DAY NEEDS?

FOR SOCIETY TO *FUNCTION*, SO MANY PEOPLE NEED TO PERFORM SO MANY ROLES WE ALL TAKE FOR *GRANTED*.

STOP! PREACHERS, STOP!

YES...?

AREN'T YOU THE ONES WHO SPOKE IN THE SQUARE YESTERDAY?

WE... WE KNOW WE CAN'T LET THINGS *CONTINUE* AS THEY ARE. WE WANT TO *HELP* YOU.

HELP US *WHAT*?

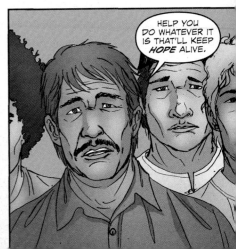

HELP YOU DO WHATEVER IT IS THAT'LL KEEP *HOPE* ALIVE.

WHATEVER YOU'RE GOING TO SAY, WALKER... THIS ISN'T THE TIME.

BUT... WHAT *NOW?* WHY DID HANNIBAL JUST *LEAVE* US HERE?

I DON'T KNOW, MAN. AND AT THE MOMENT, I DON'T REALLY *CARE.*

FASSHHH!

GABRIEL!

WE REALLY THOUGHT WE'D SEEN THE *LAST* OF YOU! WELCOME *BACK,* BRO'!

GLAD TO SEE YOU, KID.

ARE YOU *OKAY?* WHAT *HAPPENED?*

I'M FINE, BUT THE GOOD NEWS STOPS THERE.

WE'VE GOT A LOT OF *WORK* TO DO.

CONTINUED IN **DRAFTED** VOLUME 2, FALL 2008

PHOTO BY NICLAS HOLM

A Mystery In the Land of God

"The Phenomenon" has mystified scientists – and caused some to seek a more divine origin

BY M. POWERS

Jerusalem - Elan Halevi has never considered himself a spiritual man. At 23, five years in the Israeli army – the last two spent walking nightly patrols along Jerusalem's outskirts – changed him from an idealistic young soldier into what he calls "a survivor". But that all changed five days ago, when what has been dubbed "The Phenomenon" occurred.

"I didn't care anymore," relates Halevi, sipping tea in a quiet, outdoor café. "I'd been afraid for so long… and angry, I couldn't see past it. I've seen friends killed before my eyes. I've seen the immediate aftermath of suicide bombings. I knew any day could be my last, and 'my enemy' was anyone who could be a terrorist… eventually, that became any Palestinian." But Halevi's whole mindset was changed in an instant – 11: 32 PM local time, to be exact.

"I was walking patrol. Ben – my partner – was taking a cigarette break. He was talking to some young Palestinian he'd befriended. When I came to check on him, I found him collapsed, writhing in pain, with the Arab cradling him. I assumed the worst… but then, it happened to the Arab, too." His voice lowers to virtually a whisper. "And then it happened to me."

"It" was the Phenomenon, the near simultaneous - and thus far inexplicable - epidemic that occurred here the night of June 10, striking Jew and Muslim, Israeli and Palestinian alike. That it occurred during the fortieth anniversary of the Six

Day War was not lost on those who believe that a divine hand manipulated the event. "Whatever it was, it didn't discriminate," affirms Halevi. "I've talked to some Palestinians, and they felt the same thing I did. And they heard the whispering, too."

The whispering Mr. Halevi refers to is one of several symptoms that Jerusalem's denizens describe with remarkable consistency. Almost everyone this reporter spoke to agreed that the event began with what felt like a "buzzing" in their head, which grew rapidly into a pressure that seemed to build from inside. Other symptoms included hemorrhaging of the ears, nose, and in some cases, the eyes. Some swear that the buzzing sounded like someone whispering in their mind. Nothing intelligible, but a message seems to have been received nonetheless.

"It was a divine warning," Halevi states flatly. "We have to stop fighting, before it's too late. That's the bottom line."

Others are far less certain. "I won't claim to know what it was," chuckles Dr. Moshe Reiss of Jerusalem University. "But it wasn't a message from God." That opinion would seem to have been confirmed three days after the Jerusalem event – unless, of course, the Creator of the Universe has begun taking a

PHOTO BY NICLAS HOLM

special interest in St. Louis, Missouri. Just after rush hour local time, on June 13, an astonishingly similar occurrence struck the populace of the Gateway city. At approximately 7:39 PM, people across the city began experiencing intense headaches, as well as bleeding from the ears, nose, and eyes.

Significantly, there have only been eighteen reported deaths as a result of the events in both cities thus far, and all of the deceased were of advanced age. The symptoms, most agree, lasted no more than an hour, and resulted in no permanent damage. In the days since, scientists, politicians, and others across the world have postulated numerous theories as to what triggered the Phenomenon. Most scientists seem to have reluctantly settled on the idea of mass hysteria brought on by the high level of tension in the world, particularly in the Middle East.

Devon McNeil, a noted psychiatrist based in London, notes that "collective hysteria often includes religious connotations, whether overt or not." How, then, would Ms. McNeil explain the St. Louis occurrence? "That only makes the case for collective hysteria stronger," she insists. "The event in Jerusalem understandably aroused a torrent of emotion around the world. It's the center of the world's three largest religions. Billions consider it the holiest place on Earth. People simply don't understand the ability of the human mind to create physical phenomena. For instance, there are countless cases of stigmata down through the ages. What happened in Jerusalem and St. Louis is merely another example of this – albeit on a far grander scale. It's quite incredible."

Most scientists share Ms. McNeil's assessment, though some do so with less certainty. "There's really no other accept-able explanation," Dr. Reiss says. "I can't say the collective hysteria idea strikes me as being definitive. But it's the most reasonable hypothesis I've heard."

Elan Halevi, however, is certain. When told what scientists such as McNeil and Reiss have suggested in the way of rational explanations, he shakes his head. "I feel sorry for them. But before long, none of us will be able to dispute the truth. There'll be no running away. There'll be no escape."

- M. Powers

The Phenomenon:
A Gift from the Political Gods?

Five days ago, President Preston Walker's political fortunes seemed to be hopelessly on the decline. Mired in a hugely unpopular war, and with evidence of rampant corruption and malfeasance in his administration, Walker was described by some insiders as moody, depressed, and "in denial".

But that was then. Now, Walker appears reenergized. In the wake of the Phenomenon, he met with the Israeli Prime Minister in an emergency summit in Amman, and later visited a church in St. Louis. Never shy about his religious beliefs, Walker's boosters expect his piety to play well with a nervous, unsure populace. "This is his moment," one of them opines. "He was made for it. I don't know if there's a god, but if there is, he couldn't have answered our prayers any better." But not everyone is as impressed by Walker's recent activities.

"I'm appalled by his behavior, to be quite honest," says Senate Majority leader Hank Ride. "Millions of people suffered pain, nobody knows why, and he sees it as a cure-all for his own misfortunes. I think the American people – and the world – de-

President Preston Walker
Artist interpretation

serve better."

Walker's supporters, of course, scoff at this. "Obviously, Senator Ride is worried that his party's newly-won majority is going to be short-lived. The American people are behind the President all the way."

That remains to be seen. What is certain, however, is that President Walker is seizing the initiative. We can only hope that, whatever happens in the weeks to come, he chooses the high road.

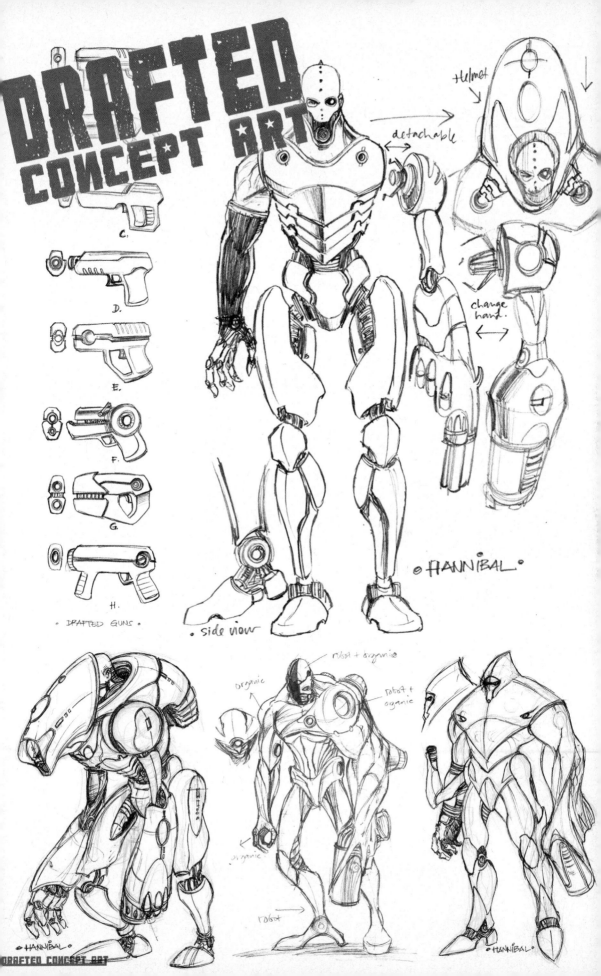

DRAFTED
CONCEPT ART

C.

D.

E.

F.

G.

H.

• DRAFTED GUNS •

• side view •

detachable

• HANNIBAL •

Helmet

change hand.

robot + organic

organic

robot + organic

robot

organic

• HANNIBAL •

• HANNIBAL •

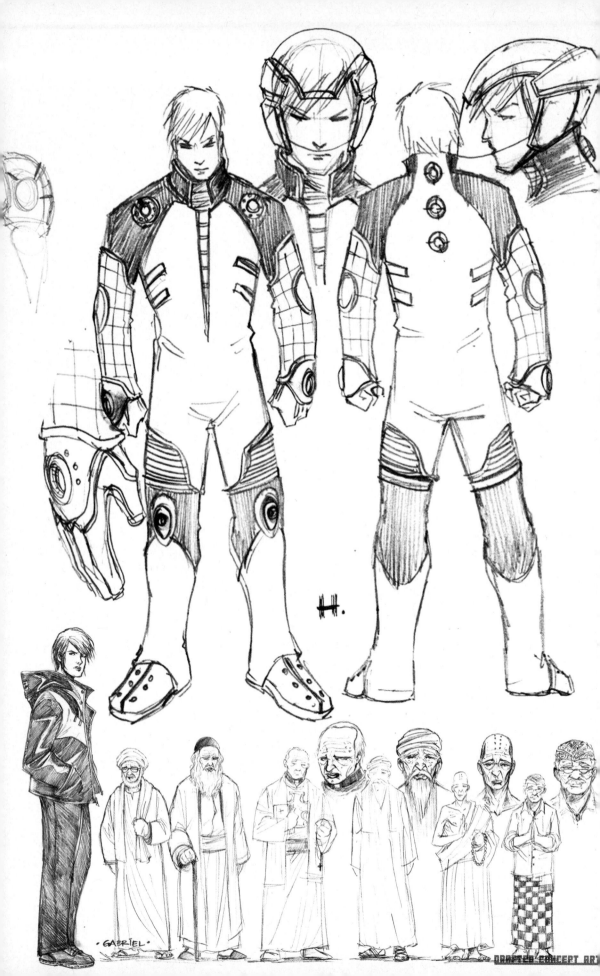

GABRIEL

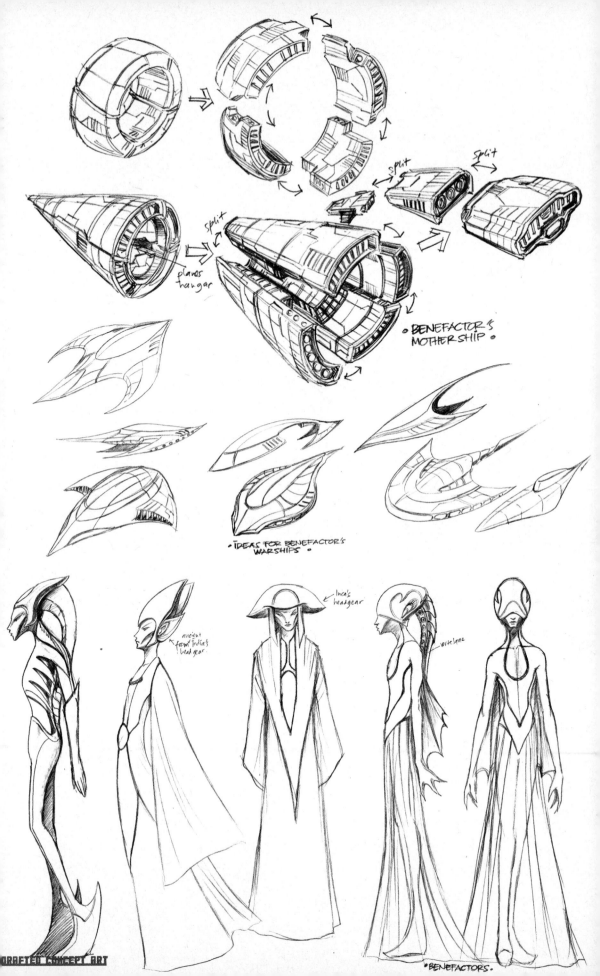

split

split

split

planes hangar

• BENEFACTOR'S MOTHERSHIP •

• IDEAS FOR BENEFACTOR'S WARSHIPS •

Inca's headgear

ancient from India's headgear.

visite lens

• BENEFACTORS •

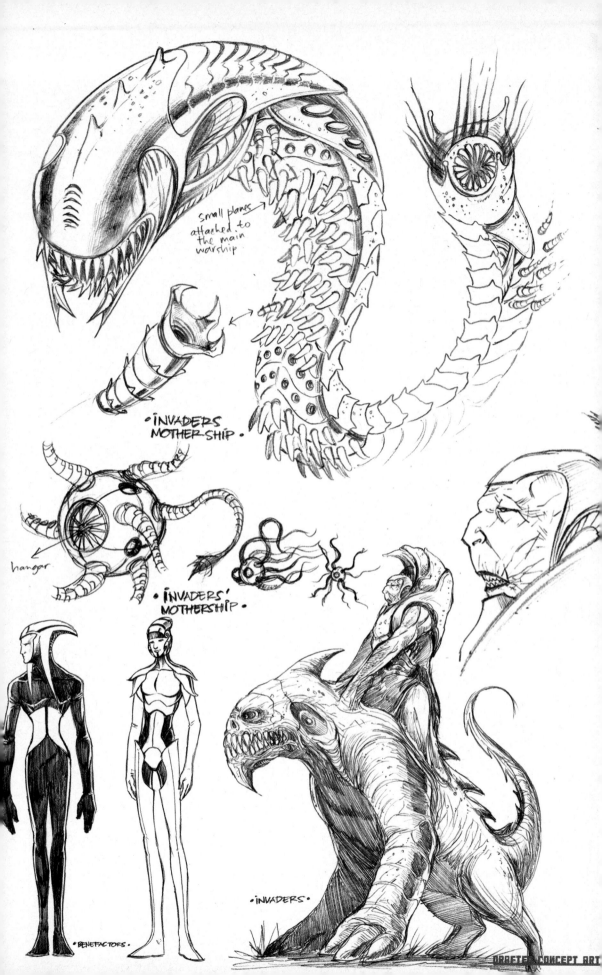

small plans→
attached to
the main
warship

• INVADERS
MOTHER-SHIP •

hangar

• INVADERS'
MOTHERSHIP •

• INVADERS •

• BENEFACTORS •

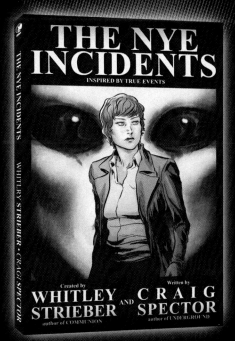

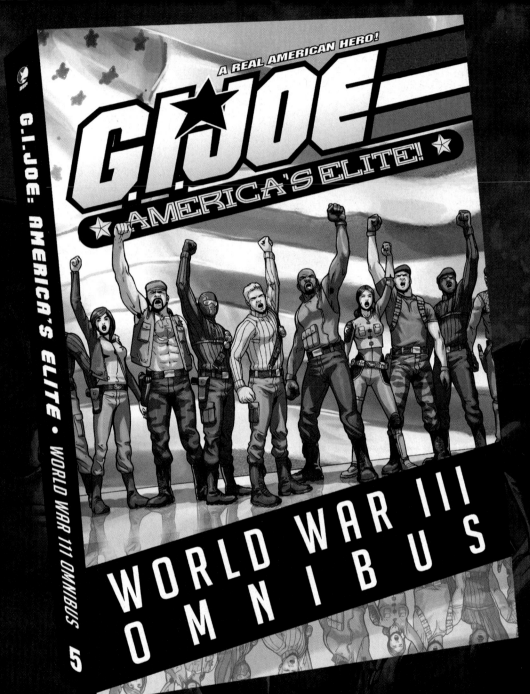